CRAZY ENOUGH TO BELIEVE IN ME

ERICA MOSELEY

Fulton Books
Meadville, PA

Published by Fulton Books 2023

ISBN 979-8-88982-582-1 (paperback)
ISBN 979-8-88982-583-8 (digital)

Printed in the United States of America

Many times in our lives, there are and will be things that we cannot seem to understand, things that make no sense, and some of these things will seem very unfair.

I am sure I am not the only person to ever experience pain or trauma, so I know some of you can relate, and a part of me feels like someone needs to hear my story.

Maybe there's someone out there who still just cannot understand why they have gone through what they have gone through. I know it sure took me a while to get to where I am today. That is, not quitting on God or myself. I was almost there, quitting, just throwing in the towel. I could not understand why God allowed me to ever breathe my first breath to begin with. Why was I brought into an experience of total hell? I wondered, *Man, why am I here if this is all I'm gonna face?*

Imagine being a six-year-old boy, and the world is just having its way with you. Then as the years go by, you start acting out. Now, all of a sudden, no one knows why you're behaving in an odd manner. They simply write you off and label you crazy. They lock you up in a mental hospital and tranquilize you, as though you are some kind of wild animal.

I just needed someone to care. I needed someone to help me, someone to protect me from the monsters in my life. But you won't find too many small children who are able to articulate that. Instead, I grew up angry, hurt, and traumatized. I did all kinds of crazy things, rebelling to try and escape my pain.

I tried everything but God.

At that time in my life, I certainly knew nothing of the significance of believing in one's self or the fact that there are times when only I will be the one to believe in me. Every day, I come to understand this a little bit more, and every day I live it.

I pray that somehow you are able to get past those horrible moments and times and that you find peace.

I was born on March 21, 1980. My mother, whom I will call Mama G, gave birth to me at Gardena Memorial. My mother had a difficult birth, nearly bleeding to death. After she gave birth to me, she was told she would never be able to have children again. I vaguely remember her saying to me at least once in my life that having a difficult birth made her feel as though I'd have a difficult life, but I didn't think much of it at the time. I guess it's not easy for a child to comprehend a mother's intuition.

The early years of my childhood went pretty well. My mother worked at an insurance company, and my father worked at a meat plant. There was also my big brother, Lulu, who was born two years before me. We don't share the same father, just the same mother. His father was my mom's ex-husband, and my father and her later met. Lulu's father was in Texas. They split, and my mom moved out to California, where she met my dad, Richard.

Things were good up until January of 1986. Things started happening—bad things. These were the things that would change my life forever.

One night while I was asleep, a loud cry woke me up. I went into Mama G's room. She was just hanging up the telephone. She was jumping up and down and screaming. "No, not my mama!" with tears coming down her face. I was only five going on six, so I really didn't know what to think or what to do, but she was scaring me. This didn't look like my mom that night. Later on, a family friend named Doris drove over and picked us up. It was Mama G, Lulu, and me. She drove us to my grandparents' home over on Lasalle. Lasalle was a street on the westside of Los Angeles, which was where a lot of my family members had been since the fifties. Most of my family were either in Los Angeles or Texas, on my mother's side.

When we turned onto Lasalle, I saw police cars. There was also an ambulance. Two men were pushing a stretcher with my grandmother lying on it. They were moving pretty fast, rushing her to the hospital. That was the last time I saw my grandmother. I was told she'd had a heart attack. Describing her, I'd say she was the kind of love you'd see at a Thanksgiving dinner.

She was a good encourager, a motivator, and she made people feel like they belonged. She was certainly a gift. It never ceased to amaze me how someone could be such a powerful presence in our lives but still be so fragile when it came to life and death.

Granny was gone.

I didn't know what this would mean for us. I had no real understanding of death. However, I could recall life becoming a nightmare.

My grandmother's name was Irene. She and my grandfather, Leonard, were a strong head of our family. Both were born in Navasota, Texas—Leonard in 1929 and Irene in 1928.

Together they had two boys and four girls: Mama G, Nee-Nee, Leonard Jr., Lamont, Marie, and Mary. From this group of aunts and uncles, I would have many first cousins. My great-grandmother, Georgia, was a full-blood Native American, and a sweet woman, so I was told. I never got the chance to meet her. She and my great-grandfather, Major, were both born in Washington, Texas. They had ten boys and one girl. Of all my grandfather's siblings, he decided to move to California with Irene in 1952.

My great-great-grandparents. Major Sr. and Mary Sweed, who were born in Washington, Texas, had three boys and six girls. My other great-great-grandparents, George and Amy Sweed, were born in Harris County, Texas. They had two boys and five girls. This was where the Sweeds met the Williams family, and it was the root of my family tree as I knew it.

In January of 1986, my grandmother left behind her part in all that history, along with a hole in the hearts of many. My grandmother was a Southern woman. Of course, she was from Texas after all. She came from the part where there were no sidewalks. From the stories I was told, back in her day, it seemed that contact with the spirits of the long gone was a common thing. I once heard that a great-aunt of mine had a spirit knock on her door, and she was so used to it that she'd say, "Come on in and sit down." If that had been me, being an eighties kid from Los Angeles, I probably would've crapped myself, then my feet would've moved faster than my shadow. Mama G was the one who told me that story. After that, I refused to sleep alone or in the dark for some time.

Now, back to my sweet ol' grandmother, and yes, she was a sweet woman. She'd always bake cakes and cookies for us children. She made sure we had money for candy when we went places like the park or on field trips. She spoiled us rotten, and boy, was she a great cook. She was a strong woman with courage, knowledge, and wisdom, who never seemed to be in a bad mood. It seemed like she had advice for any situation in life. Everyone around her looked up to her. Now, she was gone, and it appeared the happiness and love had departed along with her. It began to seem that my family was no longer family, as if everyone started to disappear. Things got really bad. At the time, I was in kindergarten, and Lulu was in second grade. When we got out of school every day at around 2:30 p.m., we'd go straight to our grandparents' house and wait there until Mama G got off work and came to pick us up. Once we got home, Mama G always made sure we finished our homework at Granny and Grandad's house.

On this one day in particular, Mom picked us up and drove us home in silence. Even though she was acting unusual, we didn't bother asking any questions. When we got home, Mom just went into her room and slammed the door. It kind of scared me. It seemed that Lulu was able to understand things better than me, maybe because he was older. As I went into my bedroom, which I shared with Lulu, I sat down on my bed and started crying. Lulu walked in and asked me, "What's wrong?"

"I'm scared."

"Scared of what?"

"I don't know, of stuff, I guess."

"What kind of stuff? Come on, Erick, you can tell me. I'm your brother."

"Well, okay. I keep having dreams about Grandmama."

"For real? What happens in your dreams? Does she talk to you?"

"No! She just stands by my bed and stares at me, then when I wake up, she's gone."

"Well, why would that scare you?" Lulu asked. "She's our granny."

I replied, "Because she's a ghost now, and ghosts scare people."

"But Granny wouldn't do anything to hurt you, so stop acting like that."

"Erick!" Mama G yelled.

"Yes, ma'am?"

"You and your brother come on and eat. I've made some fried chicken and salad for you both."

"Ooh, my favorite!" I joyfully shouted. "Thanks, Mama." I kissed her and ran off to the kitchen table and immediately started tearing apart that chicken. Stereotype or not, to this day, I still love chicken—salad also, though!

Lulu ate his up pretty fast also. Usually Mama G would make us bless our food first before we could start eating, but she just joined us at the table, quietly staring into space.

When Lulu and I finished eating, we washed our plates. Before I walked back to my room, I stopped and gave Mom a hug and said, "I love you."

"I love you too, baby," she said. I got myself ready for bed afterward.

The next morning, when I woke up, I realized my father still wasn't home. Mama G fed us and saw us off to school. However, she was now picking us up from school every day as she was no longer working. And still no sign of my father, as day after day passed by. Eventually, the phone got shut off, and the lights got shut off. We began to have less and less food. TVs and furniture began to disappear. Mom even started to disappear for days at a time.

I remember waking up early one morning, and Mom was gone. Me and Lulu had nothing to eat. There were a couple of big rats on the stove and kitchen counter roaming around. We were too scared to move, so we sat together in a corner, holding onto each other, as we just watched them. We sat cold, wearing nothing but our Fruit of the Loom underwear, for about an hour, maybe longer. Finally we worked up enough courage to run out of the house. I swear on my right arm, we both ran our little half-naked butts all the way across the street to our Uncle Junior's house. He fed us a warm meal. Mama G later came by, snatched us up, and said to Junior that she didn't want her boys over there with him. She took us back across the street to our cold, empty apartment.

I later found out that after Granny passed away, Mom and Dad had begun using crack cocaine. Actually, a few of my family members did. It took me years to put myself in their shoes, but I guessed when you lose your backbone, all kinds of bad things can happen. Mom started keeping us out of school, and we hardly ever had any food. Drugs separated Mom and Dad. One day, my dad came to the apartment demanding that she give him his son. Mom yelled, "No, he's my child. I gave birth to him. Get 'cho ass outta my house, goddammit." He grabbed my hand and took me to his car. My Mom grabbed Lulu's hand and headed toward her car, but by that time, me and Dad were at the end of the block. That was when a high-speed chase began, all the way to another side of town, to a house where his first wife and his other children lived.

Before Mama G, there was another woman. They had two girls together. Dad also had another son with yet another woman. For whatever reason, there were things the older generation refused to share with us, but I believed it was safe to say my father was all over the place.

So Mom followed us all the way there. Once Mom arrived, they argued and fought. She grabbed my arm and took me back home with her.

That's the last time I ever saw my father. Sometime shortly after that incident took place, my grandfather called the police, saying my mom was neglecting us. The next thing I knew, Lulu and I were placed in the care of our youngest aunt, Nee-Nee, in San Bernardino. We stayed with her for a while. She was only nineteen years old. She also had a boyfriend named Jeffrey living with her.

I was a rather hyperactive child at the time. I'd admit, I acted out on occasion. Jeffrey would come home drunk and beat me on a regular basis. And he'd say to me it was because I behaved so damn bad. Sometimes he was sober, and the beatings were just as bad. He even denied me food frequently and locked me in a closet as punishment while everyone else ate.

Lulu and I shared a twin-size bed, which was fine with me, so long as I still had my big brother with me. At night, Lulu would hold me in his arms while I cried until I fell asleep. Some nights, we were under sheets that were covered in my blood. Even though that was thirty-four years ago, if you looked close enough, you could see my scars.

It went on for about a year. Lulu and I were enrolled in Cypress Elementary while we lived there. One day, when we went to school, the sores hurt so badly on my legs and butt that I couldn't sit down in my seat. My teacher kept saying, "Erick, sit down. Take a seat, Erick."

Finally I said, "I can't. It hurts too much when I try to sit."

"What do you mean, sweetie?" she asked.

"My butt hurts."

She sent me to the nurse's office. A heavyset, older woman came from behind a door and softly asked me to show her where it hurt. She was very nice, and she called me hun.

I pulled down my pants, and there were scars everywhere, along with dry blood. The next thing I knew, she said, "Hold on, stay right here, I'm gonna make a phone call." While she spoke, I could see tears welling up in her eyes. Soon after, some white guy with glasses came up to me and said he was a social worker. He asked me to come with him. He promised to take me somewhere safe. I didn't know what a social worker was, but all I knew was that a white man was telling me to take his hand and to come with him.

Man, I took off running. He chased me around the school for what seemed like thirty minutes to an hour, but in real time perhaps it was only five to ten minutes. I hid under tables, by trash cans, and finally I gave up. He took me and my brother to a foster home. It was near San Bernardino, but still a good distance away.

When we got there, a porch light came on. A black woman who looked to be about forty opened the door and came to the car. The social worker (whose name I don't remember) got out of the car, came around to my side, and opened the passenger door for me. I got out, and Lulu climbed from the back seat. She smiled, hugged us, and kissed our faces.

"Hey there, little fellas," she said. "My name is Ms. Speirce. You're gonna be staying with me for a little while. Is that okay with you, darlings?"

"Yes," we both said.

"Good, then get on inside and out of this cold," she said. The social worker followed us all inside. Ms. Speirce said for us to make ourselves at home. She pointed us to the living room. She wanted to have a private talk with the social worker.

When Lulu and I went into the living room, three girls and a baby boy were all sitting around and laughing. Music was on low, and the TV was on also. The baby was on the floor crawling. He stopped and looked up at us with drool dripping from his toothless mouth. We just stayed close to each other, all shy and afraid to say anything. One of the girls spoke up and said, "Come on and sit down, y'all. Don't be scared, we don't bite. Here, give me your coats."

She took them to a hall closet. When she returned, she kneeled down in front of us so that her face was directly in front of ours, one at a time, with loving eyes. "My name is Tasha."

"My name is Erick."

"My name is Lulu," my brother answered.

"That's my sister Michelle."

"Hi, hello."

"That's Iesha."

"Hi!"

"Hi!"

"And this is little Gregory."

"Are y'all gonna be living with us now?"

"Yeah, that's what that lady Ms. Speirce said."

"How old are you?"

"I'm seven."

"I'm nine," Lulu said.

"What grade are you in?"

"I'm in the second."

Lulu answered, "The fourth."

"It's nice to meet y'all. I'm gonna be your new big sister now. Is that okay? Can I be your big sister?"

I giggled and mumbled, "Yeah."

Lulu had already sat on the floor and started playing with little Gregory. I stood next to the couch, leaning on the arm on the same end where Tasha was. She put her arm around me and said, "You can sit down. Come sit with me and let's watch TV. You like cartoons?"

"Yeah." She turned it to a channel that was showing black-and-white cartoons. It was as if everything was moving really fast, without sound. One of those really-old cartoons. I went to sit down.

"Ouch!!" I jumped back up.

Tasha asked, "Boy, what is wrong with you?"

"My sores hurt."

"What sores?"

"I got a whoopin' from my auntie's boyfriend, and it still hurts."

I started crying. She hugged me and said, "It's all right. You're gonna be okay now."

By the time Michelle and Iesha had left the room, Ms. Speirce called out, "Boys, come say bye to the social worker!" We went through the long hallway to the front door and said goodbye.

"You're gonna be safe here with this nice lady, okay?"

"Okay."

Then he left.

"You boys hungry?" Ms. Speirce asked.

"Yes!" we both responded at the same time.

"Good, I'm gonna make dinner." She told Tasha to come help her in the kitchen. Lulu went back to the living room. I stood in the kitchen between the two women as they cooked. Tasha chopped up tomatoes and rinsed and broke up lettuce, preparing to make a salad. Ms. Speirce was cleaning the chicken. By that point, she had already asked me what my favorite meal was. The two were making small talk the entire time. Then Tasha says, "Mom, you know this boy got sores all over him? He couldn't even sit down."

She replied, "Yeah, the social worker told me about it. Here, Tasha, you finish with dinner while I see what I got for his sores."

She took me into the bathroom. "Let me see your sores, sweetie," Ms. Speirce asked.

I pulled off my pants.

"Oh my lord, what kind of person does this to a little kid?"

"My auntie's boyfriend did this to me."

"I know, baby."

"He said I'd been bad."

"I don't care how bad you've been, don't nobody got no business hitting no child like they somebody slave," she said as she wiped her eyes.

She ran me some bathwater and said, "Take a bath while I find something to put on you."

As I sat in the tub, it burned at first, but I got through it. Minutes later, I got out and wrapped myself with the towel she left for me on top of the toilet. I opened the door and hollered, "I'm done!"

Nobody answered, so I went out into the hall, and Iesha was the first person I saw. She asked, "What's wrong?"

"I have nothing to wear," I replied. "Ms. Speirce put my clothes in a hamper."

"Ms. Speirce told me to give you something to wear. We're about the same size," Iesha said. "Come on."

We went to her room. She gave me sweatpants, a T-shirt, and some socks. She even gave me underwear. For the life of me, I can't remember if I actually ever wore the underwear. But I do remember going back into the bathroom and putting everything else on. It all fit perfectly. From that moment, me and Iesha became really close.

Ms. Speirce came and called me into her bedroom, where she wiped my sores down with peroxide. Then she put some kind of cream on me and wrapped me up with large bandages. Shortly after, dinner was ready.

Everyone ate chicken, salad, and buttered bread, along with some homemade juice. After, we all sat in the living room and watched a movie together. Despite it being a five-bedroom house, we all camped out together in the living room. It was nice, and it was very different from everything I was used to. Ms. Speirce's home was a loving environment. She was to this day one of the sweetest people I'd ever known.

Tasha and Michelle were her only biological children. Tasha was twenty, and Michelle was eighteen. Ms. Speirce was a foster mother to Iesha, who was a year older than me. She was also a foster mother to little Gregory too. Both of Gregory's parents were deceased. They died some sort of violent death. He was the only survivor. The decision to adopt him was still pending, as far as if the courts would grant it.

Both of Iesha's parents were addicted to drugs. That's how she ended up in a foster home.

I found out eventually Nee-Nee's boyfriend, Jeffrey, was arrested the same day that I was taken to Ms. Speirce's home. I was told that he only spent twenty-four hours in jail. When I later spoke with certain family members, they wanted nothing to do with me, saying I was a snitch because Jeffrey went to jail. They felt I had the ass whoopin's coming because I was bad. So my family washed their hands of me, as least many of them that I could recall.

Ms. Speirce enrolled Lulu and me into a school right across the street from the house. Iesha and I could never be separated since she already attended the same school.

We called each other boyfriend and girlfriend. Other people always talked about me and picked on me. They never accepted me. I had bad nervous ticks, and I flinched at almost anything (especially at male adults). The sight of them scared me.

When I was with Iesha, though, everything felt all right. She was the prettiest little girl in the world, yet she was just like me. She also didn't make fun of me or judge me. Late at night when everyone was asleep, I used to sneak into her room or she'd sneak into mine. We would get under the bed and talk for a while. She would tell me about her family, what little she could remember. I would tell her what little I could remember about mine too. We would horseplay and talk about running away together. I was seven years old, telling her I would protect her and always be there for her. One night we actually put some clothes on and left the house. It was about midnight.

We made it down the street to the darkness of an empty market parking lot. It was so dark that we got scared and ran back to the house. I had no idea where we thought we were going. I had very fond memories of Iesha.

I was able to live with Ms. Speirce for only a year. One day, Lulu's dad sent for him from Texas, and my grandfather drove from Los Angeles to take me back to Los Angeles with him. So now, me and Lulu were separated for the first time in my life.

Now it was my grandfather, his new wife, and me. He had already remarried two years after Granny's death. My stay with them was very short, but it was a long and boring time, seemingly so. It was really no more than seven or eight months. With them, all I did was go to church and school. I was always acting out, but I was never able to explain myself when asked why. I was a bit too much for Grandad, I guess, because he had me placed into a different home. This time, it appeared that I was officially all alone.

First, I lost contact with my mom, then my brother, and then everyone else I was related to. The home this time was an all-boys home. It was difficult for me to adjust there. I was one of those kids with a baby face and pretty small for my age. So at eight years old, I was much smaller than the other kids in the home. This home had some teenage boys who were the size of adult men. Two of them constantly tormented me, a list of things too.

To begin with, at that age, I couldn't figure out and I didn't have the brain to try and figure out what was going on with me, but I found myself drawn to another boy my own age. I also thought girls were pretty, but for the first time, I found myself looking at another boy in the same way I looked at girls. My mind was the mind of a child, far from sexually advanced or experienced, but as far as I understood, I wanted to be close to him, and as often as possible. Well, the two teenagers I mentioned found that pretty amusing. They teased me about it and bullied me whenever they had the opportunity to.

There was a very horrible night among many horrible nights that I could recall vividly, very vividly. They were beating me up, forcing me to perform oral sex on them, forcing me to lick their dirty buttholes. They put pencils and other objects in my behind. I was treated like this night after night, when the staff were asleep or not paying attention. Along with their actions came threats. I was told if I told anyone, they'd kill me. So in fear I didn't tell anyone. I did, however, begin acting very bizarre.

The head person in charge managed to get a mental health center to do an evaluation on me. I was prescribed multiple medications. I became zombielike because of all the meds. So much so that it was as if I forgot about the sexual abuse. Little did I find out later in life, my past, along with a bunch of emotions, would show itself in ways I wish could've been avoided.

I began getting into lots of fights. I began threatening to hurt others as well as myself. After about a year and a half, I was admitted into the community mental health center for four months (June 18, 1990, to October 4, 1990, technically, three and a half months). By this time, I was ten years of age. The chief complaint against me was as follows: "Erick is a ten-year-old black boy who was admitted for escalating behavioral problems and for feelings of sadness, fear, and suicidal verbalizations. He has had behavioral and emotional problems for about five years prior to his admission. He had been living in the foster home of Mr. Henderson."

I could go on and on with these doctors' notes because I have copies of my records, but I won't. I was diagnosed with a conduct disorder, solitary aggressive type, with an acute exacerbation. I was also diagnosed with a chronic mixed emotional syndrome, characterized by prominent feelings of anxiety and fear for my own safety. There were also feelings of anger and rage at times about not being protected. This was coupled with relatively normal childhood behavior in response to these feelings, thus generating my episodes of fighting and threatening. There was also chronic motor tic disorder, possible developmental delays, and ADHD. I was given some sort of tranquilizer, along with other medications. I was much slower than the other kids, and I never really had friends. I'd often ask staff at the hospital, "Why do I have to be locked in this room by myself?" I would say, "I don't know why I act the way I do, and for that I'm sorry."

After my time there was up, my mother's oldest sister, Mary, was given custody of me. She's probably not going to like this, but I really believed the check that came along with being my guardian made her decision very easy. I was back in San Bernardino again. I lived with Mary for a year. I must say, that year wasn't good.

There wasn't much physical abuse. The most she'd do was swat my palm with some sort of wooden paddle thing. My experience there was enough to damage me emotionally. She spent money from the checks on everything but me. She and all my relatives who were in San Bernardino treated me like an outcast. Those relatives were basically her children and their children. The adults wouldn't allow their kids to play with me or go anywhere with me, like the park, for example. They all made fun of how my nervous ticks made me shake or my eyes blink a lot. Although I was with family again, I still felt so alone.

One day, things seemed to change for me, though, in a good way. I learned that my mom was in a sober living home after completing a lockdown drug program somewhere near downtown Los Angeles. The news got even better. I was told that she'd been allowed weekend visits with me. The weekend finally came, and Mary put me on a bus by myself. The bus took me to Los Angeles.

When I got off the bus, I stood there for a couple of seconds, and I'd never forget the next thing I saw. On the opposite side of that busy downtown street and traffic jam, my mother was driving this really big green car, an old rusty thing too!

She made a U-turn and was screaming like she was all kinds of crazy. She didn't even notice the cop coming up behind her to give her a ticket, and she frankly didn't give a damn. If I remember correctly, she almost ran me over. I'm sure you can imagine someone being so excited to see me. It was probably the best thing to happen to me in a very long time. I had no idea Mama G would be so happy to see me. I didn't know she still cared. All I knew was, I had been alone for years, and I thought no one gave a damn about me. I was heavily medicated, so I was too numb to show any excitement or emotion. We made a stop at my grandfather's house, and after being there for a little while, she told me that she wanted to take me for a ride around the block. She had something she wanted to tell me. Once we were around the corner, she told me that my father had recently passed away. I simply said, "Okay," and was quiet the rest of the way.

I had no idea if I was supposed to say something or feel some type of way about it. It was as though, inside of me, nobody was home. After a couple of those weekend visits with Mama G, she was allowed to have custody of me again. She, however, had no idea how different I was compared to the sweet, playful boy she once knew. Those weekend visits were only two and a half days at a time, and there were only a couple of them. For most of the weekend visit time, she was so excited to see me again. Perhaps she hadn't noticed the changes. During those years that we were separated, she never knew in detail about most of what I endured, and I didn't know how to tell her. All she knew was that I went from home to home and that everyone said I had behavior problems. Mom didn't like how slow the medication made me act and move. Once she really took notice of it, she threw away all my medications, and she didn't renew any prescriptions. I was eleven years old, living with my mom again. She rented a small one-bedroom apartment in an area called the Jungles.

We shared the one room. Her bed was on one side, and mine on the other side. She enrolled me into Hillcrest Elementary School, where I went on to start and finish the sixth grade. She saw how much I loved basketball, so she allowed me to play for the team at the local recreation center, Rancho Cienega. I played for them for three or four summers straight. The first few years back with Mama G were actually pretty good, or normal. I graduated from Hillcrest and began attending Audubon Junior High. Besides basketball, I loved swimming, drawing, and playing video games. I was just trying to be a normal kid. At the same time, there was an awkwardness about me, to go along with the nervous tics. This gave the other kids something to tease me about. I always found myself trying to fit in or go out of my way to be accepted by my peers. I did whatever I could to get people's attention. I started pretending to be someone I wasn't. I began ditching class to show that I was cool like the other kids. I was expelled from school because I cut one too many classes. I was then sent to a different junior high school in Hollywood, Thomas Starr King.

It was kind of all right there, but eventually I behaved in a way that messed that up too with more bizarre behavior. One day, I threw away my brand-new Deion Sanders shoes right into the bushes. Then I started walking around like I got robbed and needed some help. Two Hispanic women saw me and were very worried. They were sisters, and they shared a small place together down the street from my school. They took me into their home after seeing me walking around in my socks. They asked me for my mother's phone number. They explained to her what happened, or at least what they thought happened according to me. They assured Mama G that they would take good care of me until she made it from her job, which was across town, as she was back working in insurance again. Those two sweet young ladies made me a decent meal and were both checking on me, asking if I was okay.

I was never robbed. I had been hanging out with some other kids, and I was going to get home way past the time I was expected to be home. I was afraid of the trouble I'd get in, so I made up a story. One time, I did something I knew I was gonna get in trouble for. I can't remember exactly what it was, but I was afraid of what Mom's then-boyfriend would do. He reminded me of my aunt's boyfriend Jeffrey. So while at school, I told the teacher I was scared to go home.

Social Services checked out my family immediately and questioned me thoroughly. At the end of the night, my mom was allowed to pick me up.

She was so hurt. It was my fourteenth birthday. Mama G had baked me a cake and everything. I totally ruined her surprise. When we finally made it home, with teary eyes, she took the cake out of the oven (which hadn't had the icing put on it yet) and threw it on the countertop. She couldn't bring herself to understand why I was doing the things I was doing. One day in particular, I took a BB gun to school, and I was purposely telling other students that I had it. I actually went so far as to ask a student to go tell the teacher that they knew that I had a weapon and that it was in my locker. My locker was searched, and I was arrested for the first time ever.

Later that evening, Mama G picked me up from the police station and took me home. She didn't say a word to me during the entire drive home. She just silently cried. As crazy as my actions were, I had no clue as to why I was behaving that way. After that incident, as a result, I was expelled from the Los Angeles Unified School District. It would be one year before I would be accepted into a public school again. Mama G tried private schools, but that didn't work out either.

I ended up at an alternative school, or what many would call a continuation school. This school was full of gang members, from as young as my age to people in their twenties. The school had absolutely nothing but gang members. I was the only non–gang member there. That didn't last long, however. A few of the Crips took me under their wing. I knew nothing of the ins and outs or the pitfalls of the lifestyle. All I knew was that a group of guys took a liking to me, and they all had my back. They became the place where I was a part of something. Their fights were my fights, and my fights were theirs. I had never before experienced that otherwise. Three guys jumped me in the gang one day. It was a surprise that I didn't know was coming. One guy just started fighting me. Two more jumped in, as I think he might have needed their help. I was too wild for him. Anyway, I just went with it because they seemed to care about me and they were there for me. They didn't reject me. They nicknamed me Li'l Maddog. I was fourteen at the time, and I began drinking alcohol, smoking weed, carrying weapons, fighting, selling small amounts of drugs, running away from home, stealing from people (including my own family members).

In the midst of running away, I found this shelter in Hollywood for troubled teens. I simply just didn't want to go back home. I didn't like being with my family. I didn't feel like I belonged or fit in, and I didn't feel understood.

Down the street from the shelter, I met this girl who was one year older than me. We became friends. She was a runaway too. We both wandered around Hollywood along with some other kids, looking for something to get into. One day, we were at one of her older friends' houses, who let her sleep there sometimes. It was her, a guy friend of hers, and me. The homeowner wasn't there. We were sitting in the living room, and she told me that she wanted to have sex with me. I had never had sex before, so I didn't know what to do. I just sat there quietly. I guess she felt rejected and became very angry. The craziest thing happened after that. She pulled a huge kitchen knife on me and told me to perform oral sex on her while the guy in there with us watched. First, she poured salt on her vagina then told me to go down on her. I didn't know the meaning behind the whole salt thing, but it's a true story. The part that was odd was that me and her were still friends after that. We hung out as if nothing had ever happened between us. She was still my friend in my mind. One night, we were hanging out at an apartment that was used as a drug spot with lots of gang members around. I was in one room with a couple of people, and she was in a different room with a few different people. There wasn't much going on where I was, but in the other room, they were doing PCP. She was also hanging out with one person in particular, whom she told me was "So damn fine."

Everyone stayed up pretty much all night, it appeared. I fell asleep that night. When I woke up, I went into the other room looking for everyone else. Three of them were in the room with her, with guns out. They took turns violating her. They even tried to get me to participate. They pointed guns at me and said, "Don't be a bitch. Do it." I just sat there frozen. They forced me to take my pants off, but I still never touched her. They finally gave up on trying to get me to participate. They all left the apartment together in one car. She got dressed, and I left with her. We got onto a bus together, and we rode together to a hospital. Once we got there, she was taken to a doctor. I was in a waiting area, just standing there and not sure what was next. I couldn't believe it. Two police officers came from the back and told me to come with them. They asked me to show them where to find the three guys or they would charge me with everything. This didn't make any sense. I didn't do anything wrong, I was just trying to help her, and I definitely didn't know where to find those guys. They actually took me to Eastlake Juvenile Hall, after I was booked at the police station. The DA eventually rejected the case because I did nothing wrong. By the way, on the way to the hospital, I learned she was doing things with the one guy that she liked. The other two wanted to do things with her also, but she refused, and that was when all the craziness began.

After Mama G picked me up from juvenile hall, she let me know that she understood I tried to help the girl. After only a few days of being back at home, I ran away again. First, I went back to the shelter to get my clothes. Then I went to the Eastside of South Central Los Angeles to catch up with a lot of the guys from the gang that I had become a part of. I started again with the drinking. I was committing robberies. I was partying, not going to school, and breaking into people's homes. It almost got me killed on a couple of occasions because sometimes someone would be home and they'd have a gun in hand. One guy said to me once that the only reason he spared my life was because I was a child. Me and a couple of guys were arrested one night for trying to break into a car and steal it. I was charged with attempted joyriding. I spent a couple of weeks in juvenile hall as a result.

Once I was released, I spent a little bit of time at home, then I was right back out there in the streets. I went anywhere that someone would allow me to sleep—homeboys' or homegirls' apartments, abandoned buildings and houses. One night I found a crack house. It was cold, no heat, no nothing. I saw a drug addict lying on the floor. I curled up next to her to stay warm. She didn't seem to mind. Once I found an abandoned car that was broken down. I slept in it under a big pile of clothes that were inside. I had a girlfriend named Brandy, whose mom let me sleep on the living room couch off and on. Eventually, her mom would get tired of me, and I'd leave. I remember once during 1994 Mama G couldn't deal with me anymore. She sent me to San Bernardino to stay with Nee-Nee. Nee-Nee was no longer with Jeffrey. Of course, Mom wanted me to go to a school out there and to get away from the gangs in Los Angeles. Well, after being there for only a month or so, I had an episode. Nee-Nee took a nap in the afternoon. While she was asleep, I wrote a suicide note. It read, "Don't bother looking for me because I'll already be dead." Then I left before she awoke. I went down the street to an abandoned apartment. There were no curtains on the windows, and the huge living room window was directly next to the sidewalk where someone could look right in, so I had to lie on the floor. I was small enough to do that without being noticed. There were these college age girls who lived in the apartment complex, and I told them I wasn't safe at my aunt's home. It was them who helped me hide there. They brought me food too. They ended up getting scared of getting in trouble, so they begged me to come out. Apparently Nee-Nee woke up and found the note. She called the police and my mom. Cop cars were driving up and down the street. They told people if they saw me to call them. It was on the news. Everyone was going crazy. Mama G drove up from Los Angeles as well. I didn't come out until the next morning, I believe. I was taken to a local mental health center for an evaluation and then released to my mom. She took me back to Los Angeles with her. By the way, it wasn't the typical seventy-two-hour hold. They just asked me a bunch of questions, and then they let me go. I had a lot of crazy experiences the entire fourteenth year of my life. Later that year, I lost my virginity. It's something that kind of just happened. I met a girl who was experienced and who was a part of that fast life that I was trying too hard to be a part of. When you were a part of that world, girls and sex came with it, but trust me, it wasn't healthy, loving, or fulfilling. It taught you that objectifying women was cool or even a good thing. Once that was what you learned, it was a very difficult thing to undo or unlearn. It could be some of the hardest work you would've ever done. Especially when I had so many unresolved issues with my mother, so much anger toward my mother, so much hurt caused by my mother. That would affect your trust in women. That would affect how you saw women. That bred hate and anger. You'd see your mother in all women. It didn't have to happen this way because I was aware some guys were an exception. However, when you'd have serious mental issues, coupled with internal emotions going haywire, the fog would be too thick for logic to have a place in your life.

The only thing that changed me, that helped me fight and claw my way to recovery, was time and understanding. Understanding is everything. Understanding would change you. Once you understood someone else's pain, their journey, their struggles. Once you understand how fragile we all are and that we are all only human. Mom might have been many things, but she wasn't some bionic, superwoman robot. We sometimes expected them to do more than a human being was capable of doing. When they've fallen short of a perfect mother's role, we would often make them feel like they had to live the rest of their lives bending over backward in the hopes of making things right or earning their child's forgiveness. As for me, I didn't start to understand until I was twenty-nine years old. There was a lot more that happened before that time came.

Let us continue.

Back in Los Angeles with Mama G again. Lulu moved back from Texas to live with us. So now it was Mom, her boyfriend, Lulu, and me. I forgot to mention the fact that when I was thirteen, Mama G, Granddad, and I got on a plane and flew to Texas to visit our family in Houston. I was able to spend the whole summer with Lulu. Mama G and Grandad stayed with family over in the fifth ward. I stayed with Lulu, his dad, and his stepmom in a part called Greenspoint. We'd all meet up and do things, though. My favorite was fishing and playing basketball. There was also a nice pool in the apartment building where Lulu lived. When I went fishing there in Texas, that was the first and only time I'd ever been fishing. I also remember them having a dollar movie theater.

Anyhow, Lulu was back in Los Angeles now, and we were together again. For good. Pardon me, and I apologize. It's a little difficult to remember everything in order. I'm writing this book as I recall things. Actually, when I was eleven or twelve, Lulu was put on a plane by himself to come spend Christmas with Mama G and me. Me and Lulu were so excited to see each other. We were jumping around in each other's arms and wrestling around on the living room floor. We both were unaware of each other's experiences or struggles during our years apart. We were just happy to see each other. That's all that mattered. We had on these matching pajamas Mom bought for us. That Christmas will always be a highlight for me. Okay, so now back to the year Lulu moved back to LA to live with us. It was pretty cool to have my brother back now, but unfortunately we were headed in two completely different directions. I was already so trapped in the darkness of my mind. I learned that Lulu was gay. I wondered why he was gay. I didn't really understand much about being gay. I often made little jokes that got on his nerves sometimes. One time, I put his small male cheerleaders' shorts on, walking around the house imitating him a comical manner. When his gay friends would come over to the house, I would be nervous around them and try to avoid them. Little did anyone know, I was already very confused about my own sexuality.

No matter how hard I tried, I just could never get to the point where I was sure of myself. I couldn't tell anyone, but as a teen, I always had the same self-consciousness issues I heard girls talk about. At least some of them anyway. I especially wore baggy pants to hide my butt. That would sound funny coming from a guy, right? There wasn't a time in my life where I felt masculine. I was always careful to pay attention to how I walked, because when I left my guard down, people would say I walked like a faggot. So I did my best to fit in. I went out of my way to maintain the approval of my peers. My discomfort and nervousness around gays and transgenders, in hindsight, was because I feared they'd see right through me and expose me. Instead, I continued to be all over the place. I continued drinking on a regular basis. I was having a lot of sex partners, and I made sure all the guys knew about it. I didn't want them to see me as anything other than just like them.

I continued to run away from home for a little while. When I was fifteen, I went to a lockup camp for five months for burglary (Camp Kilpatrick). While there, I learned that Mama G's then-boyfriend, Matthew, put his hands on her, and that they were no longer together. I was told that he left town. She soon after met another man. His name was Eric, just like mine (without the *k*). Everyone called him Speedy. Speedy had a daughter, who was two years younger than me. To this day, Speedy and Mama G are still together. He, too, was a recovering addict, just like Mom. I guess things would work out a lot better when you could relate to your mate because y'all share common ground. Around the way, they called it cut from the same cloth. While I was in camp, Mom, Speedy, and his daughter came to visit me. I remember handing his daughter a letter. In the letter, I told her how I always wanted a little sister. Her name was Terri, by the way. It felt like things would be okay. You know what I mean. It seemed as if we would all be one big happy family.

When I was released from camp, I was enrolled into Lincoln High School in Lincoln Heights. Not too far from East LA. This was my first time in a public school since I got in trouble for bringing a weapon to my junior high school. At Lincoln High, I made the junior varsity basketball team. I was actually doing okay. I made it through the entire school year. I wasn't the star of the basketball team or anything like that. I didn't get much playing time either, but I stayed with it. I attended summer school as well. I practiced basketball every day after school with my teammates over the entire summer. I got better and better. Speedy and Terri moved in with us. We were all cramped into a tight space, but we were all together as a family. I was asked by the girls' softball coach if I would help out with all the equipment. I was able to travel with them to all their games. This made me feel pretty good and responsible.

At one point, I believe when I was sixteen, Mom put me in acting school. I had a mentor also. A lot of people were trying to help me. As usual, a day came when I would sabotage it all.

My mentor really tried too. He took me to a bunch of positive, informal, and educational places, trying to show me a different side of life. No one knew I needed some serious healing. Not even I knew. In my situation, all the beautiful, shiny Band-Aids in the world wouldn't have done any good. I was introduced to successful people. I was taken to places that taught me about my history. I was taken to sporting events. Nothing touched me the way it was intended to.

I ran away once more. I was arrested a couple more times for having contact with gang members. It was a violation of my probation. I did so well for a little while when I stayed away from the gang members. Regardless as to how good I did at times, I always threw it away. Mama G admitted to herself that I was unstable. She took me to a therapist, and I said that everything was fine. I told the therapist there was nothing I wanted to talk about. I said I didn't have any problems and life was good. I wasn't ready to talk yet.

She never took me to talk to a therapist again. I wouldn't say that I was lying or pretending. It was more like my true feelings were buried inside my subconscious mind, and I didn't know how to locate them. At that point, Mom still didn't know the specifics of what I went through on a day-to-day basis while we were separated.

It was as if I didn't remember the things that happened to me. There were numerous times I'd be somewhere alone. I'd feel an overwhelming sadness. I'd be crying, and I'd feel as if I had no one in the world who was really on my side. Even if it wasn't literally true, in those moments I felt totally alone in the world. It was as if a spirit or a being whose name was pain or darkness would smother me when it caught me by myself. I was paralyzed by it, and I didn't know a way out. I was often distant with my family. During family pictures, I'd be the only one not smiling and disengaged. During family gatherings, sometimes I'd go off somewhere by myself staring into space. Sometimes someone would find me and ask me what was wrong, and I'd say "Nothing" or "I don't know." At times, my mom complained that I hardly ever seemed interested in participating in things with the rest of the family. I started to simply shut down.

I also started having confrontations with different family members. So when I ran away for the last time, I was missing school and getting in trouble with gang members once again. I went to juvenile hall a couple more times for petty violations. I had to go back to continuation school again. Two different schools, actually, up until I was seventeen years old. Once the summer of 1997 was over, I was able to enroll into Dorsey High. For the first time, I actually made the football team as a receiver. I missed too many practices, so the coach didn't give me playing time. Until one day I finally quit the team.

By the time I went to Dorsey, I was completely avoiding gang members. I realized they weren't my friends, not real friends. A couple of them teamed up on me one day and stole things from me. They put me down and made fun of me. They even questioned my sexuality. Over a couple-year span, they noticed how different I was from them. It became too hard to keep up with the act, I guess. So now I totally avoided them. As far as I was concerned, they were no longer my homies. They went from treating me like a little brother to treating me like an outcast. Thankfully, we didn't live that close to them at this time, so I hardly came in contact with them. I definitely didn't go anywhere near the neighborhood they hung out in. I kept trying to do the right things, and for at least a little while, I was able to live and behave like a normal youngster: sports, high school, video games, skating rink, going to the movies, swimming, and playing football in the middle of a residential street with other kids.

When no one was around, I had some other things going on with me, however. I'd put on female clothing items and look at myself. I began feeling more and more things for guys. I couldn't understand it, and I for sure never shared it with anyone.

When I saw beautiful women, I envied them. To be like the other guys in the environment I was in, I had a bunch of girlfriends, trying to be some type of player or slick-talking dude. It was all a front. Looking back at it, it was even deeper than that. I used to go from girl to girl, breaking up and moving on without explanation. I believe this was my way of leaving them before they had a chance to leave me. Now that was what I'd call some serious abandonment issues.

To a degree, I still have abandonment issues. Even though I have people in my life, I still feel like the possibility of being completely alone looms over me, though it's been decades since my childhood experiences. Overall, I didn't know how messed up I was or how badly I needed some help. I had no idea at the time that I was acting out, asking for help. I had no idea that finding a way to or trying to talk about it is the only healthy way to deal with trauma. I didn't know that if I kept it in, things would come out in an ugly manner.

All the times I'd gotten into trouble, it was never anything very serious, like physically hurting someone. Unfortunately, that all changed. Late 1997, when I was still seventeen years old, I hurt two people very badly. When I was arrested in early 1998, I went through the court process, and I was sentenced to life in prison. I never thought I'd ever do something like that. If you would've asked me beforehand what I thought of people who hurt innocent people, I most likely would've have told you these people are filth or scum.

Once I was taken to juvenile hall, I was placed on suicide watch, and they gave me some type of medication. At the police station, when I was left alone in the interrogation room, I took my shoestring out of my shoe and tied it in a knot around my neck. An officer saw me through one of the two-way mirrors, and several officers rushed in and were wrestling with me in order to remove it from my neck. That's how I ended up in suicide watch. I was only there for a few days.

I had been to juvenile hall many times before, but this time it was different. I was housed in a high-risk-offender unit. My unit in particular housed some of the worst kind. It was so embarrassing, and I felt very ashamed. Some of the staff didn't have a problem with constantly reminding me about the nature of my crimes. One staff member told me I was the lowest person in the world and all the bad things that would happen to be when I got to prison. Well, I didn't need to be reminded how horrible of a person I was; I already knew it and felt it. Mama G visited me a couple of times in the juvenile hall. After five months, I was transferred over to the men's central jail, three months after my eighteenth birthday. While I was in the men's central jail, Mom never came to visit me. She told me it was because of her past record. (While going through the worst part of her addiction, she went to prison.) Mom never came to any of my court appearances. She told me she couldn't sit through it. It was too much for her. Before the courts proceedings went too far along, the DA had two mental health doctors come to speak with me. They asked a bunch of simple questions. Things like if I knew what time it was, the date, the day, the month, if I knew my name, and if I understood the words they were saying. It lasted no longer than thirty minutes. I believe the DA had them ask me basic questions, and they said I was competent to stand trial.

Back to when I was still in juvenile hall, I could recall kids as young as fourteen and fifteen being tried as adults and facing the rest of their lives in prison. I was around lots of youngsters whose lives were most likely over before they even had a chance to understand life. During most of my court hearings, I put my head down and did my best to tune out everything that was said. I asked my public defender for a pen and a notepad. I would just write things down. I didn't want to listen to it, and I tried very hard not to hear it. I felt awful with the entire courtroom looking at me. It was humiliating.

So anyway, back to my transition from juvenile hall to the men's central jail. I had previously heard stories about the county jail, so I was pretty scared. The sheriff had no idea that I was eighteen (the one who worked in processing). He thought that I would be going to the juvenile floor they had there. Even though the juvenile hall had units for those of us who were charged as adults, the county jail also had a floor for us as well. So at first I was kept away from the adult men and told to go sit on the other side, where the women were being processed.

The women were looking at me all worried like a bunch of mothers. They were asking me questions like "Boy what did you do? You look so young, why are you in here?" I just put my head down and wouldn't talk to anyone. After a while, a deputy came across my information and yelled out, "You're eighteen! Get over there with the men down the other way." I came to a row of holding cells with a bunch of grown men who looked like hardened criminals looking for trouble. I didn't say anything to anyone. I just found somewhere to sit alone. I became invisible while everyone talked among themselves. Nobody bothered me. Hours later, I was processed. A nurse asked me if I was feeling okay.

She also asked if I was feeling suicidal. My answer was yes. I was then placed on a seventy-two-hour suicide watch. It was a cell with a big glass door. The staff could see me without anything being in the way. Where they sent me was across the street from men's central jail. It was twin towers. Not the actual Twin Towers. That's what they called that jail. Twin towers was more of a medical facility for inmates with health concerns or mental health issues. Maybe just mental health, I can't remember. I was in twin towers for two months. Once the seventy-two-hour suicide watch expired, I was sent to a different floor there instead of men's central jail. Everyone in this unit was taking psychiatric medication. It was mostly older guys, so it was laid-back. But there was this one guy who was twenty-five or twenty-six that I got into a fight with during a game of basketball. Once a couple of months passed, I was moved across the street to men's central jail. It was way more rowdy over there. I saw a lot of violence there. There were gang rapes, people dying, you name it. In the county jail,

I was introduced to pruno (homemade alcohol). I'm not going to lie, I enjoyed the distraction from my sorrows. There was so much tension between Blacks and Hispanics there that as soon as I got there, one of the guys told me he thought it was best if I kept something on me that I could defend myself with because they'd likely try to catch me by myself.

Thankfully, during my time there, none of those sort of situations ever came to pass. Other than one fight, where I was defending myself, I made it through the county jail experience just fine. I guess getting drunk and getting into an occasional fight was the new normal for me. Let me just say the medical system was horrible in the county jail in 1998. You never know, maybe it's gotten better and maybe not. One day I ate some jalapenos that were sold in the commissary, and later that day, I started breaking out in hives all over my body. That had never happened to me before, so I was scared to death. I told the deputies that I needed to see a nurse or doctor, but they just dismissed me. So I went down and said I was dizzy. The other inmates told me that was what it took to get some medical attention, so that was what I did. Two inmates carried me all the way to medical. First, the deputies tried to make me walk, but I kept falling down. The nurse gave me an antibiotic injection, and the next morning the hives were all gone. When I realized what kind of place jail was, I felt like I couldn't walk alone. I reassociated myself with gang members. In here, they have your back, and you have theirs. Everyone's hooked up to something. Blood, Crip, Muslim, Christian, and the other races have their own thing.

One of the things I really disliked about prison was it took your humanity away, if you'd ever had any to begin with. It made it hard for you to maintain the ability to communicate with and understand a variety of people. In prison, it was only eat at the same table as your own, use only these showers, use only these phones, play basketball with your own, exercise with only your own, be cellmates with only your own. The officers' objective was to keep their foot on your next. They were the enemy. Every other race was your enemy. Even your own could become your enemy if you pissed them off or disagreed with them. This was what I was surrounded by when I came to prison as a teenager. These were my conditions. This was what I would have to counter, if I was to ever have a chance at becoming a mature, decent human being. It's safe to say it was an almost-impossible task. Luckily almost wasn't absolute.

I was transferred to a prison reception center in February of 1999 with a life sentence. This was one month before my nineteenth birthday. Not a lot went on in the reception center besides a big riot between Northern Mexicans and Southern Mexicans. The tower officer was shooting at them. At the time I didn't know there was a difference as I thought it was an actual gun. Turns out they were shooting a block gun. I was literally feet away from all this. It gave me a taste of what I would see in prison. (By the way, block guns are nonlethal.) Once I was housed in a regular prison, I began seeing things that scared me and humbled me. My years on level 4 prison yards gave me a glimpse of what it was to be surrounded by evil, perhaps more than a glimpse.

When I saw the stabbings, and someone collapsing from all the hits from the shanks, I wished quietly in those moments I could be back in the safety of my mother's home. The times I felt backed into a corner until I did things I didn't want to do, I wished there was a way I could get away from it all. But I couldn't. I also understood very well that not a soul was coming to save me. I had no choice but to adjust and do whatever it took to never be anyone's victim or everyone's enemy. No one knew how scared I was. No one knew about the tears when the coast was clear. No one knew about the poems written to God, crying out for his mercy, and though it seemed in vain, I kept on writing.

As a kid, I had seen people beaten, shot, and stabbed right in front of me. I'd even survived a couple attempts that were made on my life, but I had never seen anything like that riot. There were so many people. I knew from that point that anything could happen to me in prison around these kinds of people. Although I clicked back up with the gang, I always felt and knew deep down inside they didn't give a damn about me. All that having my back and stuff was mostly out of obligation for the sake of the gang and to establish and maintain a certain reputation. Once in a while, you'd encounter someone who cared a little bit, but it was very uncommon. If and when you'd take a step back and start paying attention to things and analyzing things, you'd come to the conclusion that, sadly, you were alone.

This is your own journey, and perhaps in a way, you must journey alone without distraction to figure you out and to figure out a thing or two about life. For my first several years, I wasn't afforded much opportunity to do anything productive or accomplish anything. I was placed into a GED class, but I could never invest any real time into my work because we were always on lockdown. This made going to class a here-and-there kind of thing. Also, when I was in class, I struggled with being able to concentrate. I would get confused trying to process all the information. Basically, everything going on was not a good recipe for success.

Lockdowns were very common in the higher-level, maximum-security prisons. The longest lockdown I'd ever been on lasted for one year: Lancaster prison, from the summer of 2002 to the summer of 2003. When it lasted that long, it was usually because an officer or officers had been attacked. From my experience, the lockdowns didn't last that long when it was inmates versus inmates. Perhaps we were not as important or valuable. So during that one-year lockdown, I was forced to sit with my thoughts twenty-four hours a day. In that small cell, my past took that time as an opportunity to pay me a visit. At this time, I was twenty-two years old. All the abuse I experienced came back to me. All the beatings, the neglect, and the molestation. It all came together. I said to myself, *Now I know why I'm so messed up.* I realized I repeated some of the same things that were done to me. I felt as if I was no better than the people who had hurt me. As I mentioned earlier, I hurt two people when I was seventeen years old. The most I could say was that they were aged fifteen and twenty-eight. I was advised not to mention much in detail. Up until that point, I had been trying to figure out why I was so messed up. When it hit me, it came like a ton of bricks. It was too much for me to handle, so I found a solution. I came to the conclusion that I hated myself and that it was best if I was no longer alive. I felt I was too damaged, and there was no point in taking up any more space in the world. I decided to end it all. I had fifty or sixty 500 mg pain pills. I also had some pruno. I drank a quart of pruno while swallowing the pills a few at a time. I had my headphones on, listening to my Discman, and I laid back on my bunk. My plan was to fall asleep, a deep, dark sleep, never to return to this world. Later that night, I woke up and immediately was pissed off at still being alive. I pretty much threw up off and on for the rest of the night. It was as if something inside me was pushing the ills out of my body. My cellmate (who was on the bottom bunk) had no idea that I was on my top bunk swallowing all those pills. When I kept throwing up, he assumed pruno made me sick. I never told him it was a suicide attempt.

For the next couple of days, I was pretty sick. I couldn't keep anything down. Anything I ate came right back up. Even when I tried to drink water, it came back up. I had no idea such a thing was possible. During those two days, I was miserable. When I finally saw a medical staff walking by passing out medication, I told her something was wrong with me. I explained that I hadn't been able to keep anything down for a couple of days. The guards handcuffed me and took me to the infirmary. Coincidentally, at the time, there was a stomach bug going around, so the medical staff assumed that was all it was. They gave me an injection that was meant to settle the stomach, and it worked like a charm. I will say, though, for the next several years, I had pain that came and went in the area of my kidneys. With my suicide plan failing, I was forced to face the demons of my past. I tried to run from it, but I couldn't. I was trapped. I basically had to face it and deal with it. There was no escaping it. Next, I wrote a letter to Mama G and spilled my guts. I said to her, "Mom, I'm not trying to make you feel bad, but these are the things that happened to me while you were on drugs." I told her how I was treated by people, how I was beaten, molested, denied food, bullied, how I was an outcast, and so on. I said, "Mom, this is why I'm so messed up." At first it seemed as if Mama G held back to a degree because of the nature of my offenses and because of how much trouble I caused her. I believe it was safe to say I had become a lost cause. I didn't and I hadn't given anyone a reason to believe in me. I remember once when I was seventeen, something I heard in class prompted me to ask Mom if she'd been saving any money for me to go to college. She flat out told me "No." She said it was because I had never given her the impression that I cared about going to college. She, along with others, told me they thought I wouldn't be alive long enough to go to college. Everyone around me believed I would die before eighteen.

So fast forward to the letter, after the failed suicide attempt, Mom wrote me back, and she seemed to have some understanding now. She told me about how sorry she was for not being there. She told me how she wished she could've been there, she wanted to, but her addiction had a grip on her. She tried to explain to me about how I should forgive myself, how I could start the process of forgiving her. It all was based on me praying to God and opening up more. She told me how God could help me. She told me that once I became the man that God wanted me to be, he'd turn my circumstances around and grant me a second chance. I knew she meant well, but I definitely couldn't wrap my mind around the possibility of a second chance. As far as I was concerned, my life was over. I also didn't have much time to deal with or focus on my feelings. My life was all about survival. When the prison wasn't on lockdown, I had to constantly be alert. All day, there was so much to watch out for and be aware of. No lie, not paying attention to your surroundings at all times could cost you your life. I was on level 4 yards (highest level of maximum security) for my first seven years.

Once I went down to a lower level, things changed a whole lot. First of all, to get to a lower level, you have to go without getting write-ups long enough for your points to go down. I was able to do that. When I went to a lower level, besides when I first got there, I never again saw another stabbing or riot. Not saying that it never happened on lower-level yards, just that I hadn't seen it. Back to what I was saying. In lots of ways my past still affected me. Also, the confusion about my sexuality came back, and it came back strong. Oh, and do you remember when I talked about all the crazy stuff I did when I was in junior high (taking my shoes off, walking around acting like I was robbed)? Well, this was embarrassing, but I wanted to share with you something that probably would take the cake.

In my head, I felt that nobody really cared about me. For a long time, I felt what support I did get from my family was to make themselves feel better, to make it to where they could sleep at night. It was for their own conscience. I just couldn't imagine it being because someone actually loved me. For I don't know how long, I couldn't love me, so how could anyone else? In my early twenties, this was what I did. I was already tired of prison, and I decided I would find a way to kill myself, and this time I wouldn't fail. The timeline I gave myself was ten years. Altogether, I was only gonna do ten years in prison. Once ten years came, I would commit suicide. But before I left this earth, I wanted to experience love for the first time. Unconditional love, undivided attention, and someone's quality time. I figured maybe get more of my family members to write me letters, visit me, and be there for me overall. I felt so lonely. Mom and I were getting kind of close, but still, she was always so busy. That made it impossible for me to see her as often as I'd like (visits), and she'd never been much of a letter writer. So in order to get attention, I told my family that I had cancer and that I only had a few years to live. I thought they would feel bad for me and be in my corner 100 percent. Do you want to know what they did? Exactly what they were already doing up until that point. Now that really made me feel even more like I was nothing. I was young, you know. Now, as I reflect back, I see that. I loathed myself, and I didn't think I was good enough as I was. I couldn't manage to accept myself, so I looked for others to make me feel better about myself. As an adult, I was still an insecure, emotional little boy. I tried everything I could think of to feel better about myself, because truth be told, I couldn't stand my black ass. I hated my guts, and I hated mirrors, so I looked everywhere else, so long as it was outside of myself. I tried everything under the sun. Everything except God.

In 2007, it occurred to me that I'd never seriously considered the possibility of God being able to make a difference in my life. When that truth hit me, everything changed. I begged God to heal me, and to be honest, I could say now that God works wonders. However, at the time, I was naive, and I thought change was supposed to be instant, like magic. I was unaware I would still have to travel down a long, bumpy road, and that I wasn't gonna come out of this unfazed, or untouched. I asked God to come into my heart, to cleanse me. I asked him to make me a new man, to have mercy on me, and to give me one last chance at life. I hoped that I didn't have to remain hopeless and that I didn't lose the rest of my life based on a mistake I made as a messed-up kid. I was willing to listen and learn, whatever it took to become a real man, and a good man. I also prayed that if by chance this is my fate, no matter how sorry I was, God would have mercy and take me to my grave. In April of 2007, I was baptized in the prison chapel. I was going to church regularly. In December of the same year, I got my GED. I guess finally I was able to concentrate hard enough to accomplish that. Of course, not without the help of a patient tutor. I was so happy to achieve something good. The education department put on a real graduation and everything. Mama G was allowed to attend the graduation. I'd tell you that was the first time in my life where my mom looked at me with a proud look in her eyes. I'd never forget the feeling. I didn't know that I could make someone so proud of me. I just started to believe I could do this and I could do that. I at least had to try as far as I am concerned. I had something to prove to myself as well as others.

I began to feel like a responsible adult. I was so busy doing positive things that I didn't have time to sit around with any gang members. An old high school girlfriend even came back into my life in 2008. She came to visit me more than anyone ever had at that point. We wrote each other lots of letters, and we talked on the phone every single day. I believed that a man and woman was the only thing that was right and the only thing God would approve of. Before she came into my life, I had had a few experiences with other men. It was three guys between 2003 and 2005. It was something I was up and down, back and forth about. In 2007, I started praying about it. I told God that I wanted to be who he wanted me to be. I asked him if he would take the desire out of my heart. I didn't want to continue struggling with my sexuality. I wanted to live a normal life. I wanted a wife, and I wanted kids (once free, of course). I started believing I was gonna get out of prison someday.

No matter how much I tried to pray it away, my desires never went away, and my deep-down feelings never changed. Even with a lovely woman in my life, I still felt something opposite going on inside of me. I never felt like a normal guy. I never felt like I was one of the guys when I was among other men. To fit in or to be like them was a task. It did not come naturally. I was always more emotional and sensitive about things, and I had to hide it because it was prison. I thought having a girlfriend would help me to get rid of my homosexual feelings, but that didn't work. Whenever gays or transgenders were around, I had to avoid them because I felt things. It was energy. I definitely wouldn't let them know what was going on with me because their loudmouth asses would make sure everyone knew the "T," as they called it. Let me tell you, you don't know what messy is until you're surrounded by a bunch of gays and trans women. Oh, and please keep reading before anyone gets offended. So my relationship with the old high school girlfriend only lasted for a year. When our relationship was near an end, a really bad case of depression came over me. She had her own problems, so she definitely couldn't handle mine. She pretty much disappeared. It was pretty devastating at first, because I hated being alone. I'll be honest, that pain led me to hurt myself again. I went days with no food and a couple days without water. I had a buddy named Ed who talked me into eating and drinking again.

Let me back up a moment. In 2007 when I got saved, the lie I told my family about me having cancer began to eat away at me. I felt really guilty, so I confessed in a letter to Mama G. To my surprise, the only thing she was concerned about was if I would still kill myself once the ten-year mark came. I told her no, I wouldn't kill myself. And obviously I still hadn't killed myself, but over the years, I'd still engaged in self-harm. Depression is one tough SOB. Trying to be who everyone else thought I should be started killing me inside. Being around the chaplains, who talked about their children and wives. Other men in the prison, whose wives and children visited them. I felt like I had to be like them. I felt like that life was normal and traditional. Only God and I knew my inner struggles. However, I wasn't able to continue carrying on in that kind of way. Between still being affected by my past, confusion about my sexuality, the self-hate and guilt, the depression, and the thoughts in my head became overwhelming. I couldn't take it anymore. I went to talk with a psychologist. I broke down crying. I told her about my whole life. I told her about all the bad choices I had made. That conversation I had with her was the first time I opened up about the suicide attempt from when I was twenty-two years old. I told her that I felt no matter how good of a person I can become, no matter what I could go on to accomplish in my life or how much I changed, there would always be these animal-like things that I did that I can't take back or erase.

I told her I would give my life to be able to go back and take away the things I'd done. I didn't mention anything about my sexuality. I only discussed my childhood experiences and the crimes I committed. She explained to me that with help from the mental health program, and with time, I could get better. I could heal from the inside out. She said it appeared I had never opened up to anyone who could help me. She said opening up was a big step, and it was the beginning of healing, but I had a lot of work to do. I was twenty-nine years old at the time. At twenty-nine years old, I was finally ready, and desperate enough to do whatever it took to be better and in a place where my past no longer dictated my life and how I felt and acted. I was placed in the enhanced outpatient program (EOP), which was one of the highest levels of mental health services in prison. The only thing above it was being in a department state hospital. In the EOP, there were hours and hours of groups, one-on-one therapy sessions with your psychologist, and recreation therapy with RTs so you could learn to interact with others in a healthy way. There were always check-ins and people checking on you. If you were really actively participating and doing the program, basically serious about getting help, the staff were really very supportive. If you were willing to go all in, they'd also go above and beyond for you, as far as the time they put in with helping you versus the inmate patients who weren't serious and just go through the motions. I can't tell you how many times I was told by a mental health staff that it was nice to be working with a patient who was serious or for real about wanting help. Up until that point, I blamed other people for the way my life turned out. It was because of what everyone in my life had done to me. If it wasn't for my mother using drugs and leaving me, none of this would have ever happened. I wouldn't be so damaged and have all these problems. If it wasn't for all the people who have hurt me, I wouldn't know how to hurt other people, and I wouldn't have it in my heart. I never once looked at myself or considered the possibility of me somehow being responsible. It took me being embarrassed and humiliated in a room full of professionals to really get my attention.

When I was first put into EOP, I had to go to a meeting with all the main mental health staff, who would have me on their caseload. It was several staff members, along with my correctional counselor. When the subject of my crime came up, as usual, I did the blame game. One of the female staff members let me have it, more blunt and harsh than anyone ever had. She told me how I couldn't blame anyone but myself. She told me I needed to accept responsibility and stop pointing the finger at someone else. Don't get me wrong, my feelings were hurt, and she made me cry, but up until that point, that was the realist shit I'd ever been told. Later in my cell, it occurred to me that I really needed to take a look at myself. A good long, hard look. I had slice of humble pie that day.

Soon after that, I had a one-on-one therapy session with a female social worker, and boy, was she also very honest. I told her my story, and she gave me or shared with me her wisdom. She explained to me the road would be difficult but that it was possible if I was truly serious. She kept it real about my having to perhaps go above and beyond in order to make things right. She pointed out to me that I would have to live the rest of my life trying to make it right, or right my wrongs. One of the most important things she advised was doing what I could to help people who have been victimized by violence. I took her every word to heart. I embarked on a journey I could never forget. I pointed out that the two individuals I just mentioned were women because of its ironic nature.

Most of the psychologists, psychiatrists, social workers, rec therapists, teachers, tutors, friends, pen pals had all been women. The very ones I had an unhealthy view of, ill-feelings toward, scared I was never good enough for, always feared they would turn their back on me, wanted to hurt them before they hurt me, the very ones whom all I've offended and mistreated, they'd listened, they'd understood, they'd believed my sorries and showed me the way. Their compassion had taught me to feel compassion for others. Their patience had given me patience. They taught me how to love. They showed me how to forgive others as well as myself. They molded me and shaped me into being human. I now cared about what was going on in the lives of others versus wanting everyone to stop what they were doing and tend to my needs. I'm saying I fully understand that many, many people suffer, some worse than me, and they still hadn't gone out harming innocent people. There's no excuse for that, and I get that now. I was not alone in my suffering. Sometimes we all suffered in some sort of way. It appears to all be a part of the human condition and experiences. There's a much better way to go about things, one that's better for everyone, where no one's life has to be negatively impacted. It sounded so easy and simple. I guess I must've been a really slow kid. It was called talking, even if it was difficult to articulate my deepest feelings and concerns. As a kid, I wish I could've at least said I was hurting inside. I was sure that would've been enough to make a therapist dig deeper. Too bad there was not much that could be done about the past. It was, however, a huge relief knowing I could live out the rest of my existence in a much different manner. Life is beautiful when you awaken from your stupor. When you learn the difference that talking makes, weakening the power of the poisons in which were grown by the past.

I was not so sure the scars will ever heal 100 percent, but there will definitely be room for new information. There would be room for the reprogramming of one's self. For seven years, therapy sessions and groups were my life. Listening, watching, reflecting, pondering, and paying attention. Paying attention is very important because the universe will always speak to you and reveal things to you if your path is of good intention. I asked for a second chance, for forgiveness, and for healing. My helpers were the ones I assumed would loathe me and spit on the reality of my existence. I'm still amazed by that. I have been so embraced I can't believe it. I realize this is something in my heart I've always wanted, to be embraced. I didn't know this or have a good enough sense of self to understand this before.

I had no idea that having the right kinds of people to surround me would turn my life around in the way that it had. In knowing this, now all I'd accept into my life was the right kinds of people. Another thing that really helped me to reprogram myself was books. Books awoke a deepness inside of me. Powerful words and messages were something my spirit wouldn't allow me to ignore. Once my eyes were opened to other possibilities—other truths, purity, compassion, forgiveness of self, and others—there was and is still no turning back. Emotionally and spiritually, I'd been to faraway places. I didn't get what I needed from my upbringing or former surroundings. The universe and all that was good took me into its wings and gave it to me one spoon at a time. However, there were certain areas of my life where I remained naive, perhaps well into my thirties. I assumed I wouldn't suffer any more pain in my lifetime. I came to the conclusion that I'd survived things that the average person wouldn't survive. I felt like God would protect me from any more suffering. I thought I had already taken the best or harshest blow life could throw, but I was wrong. I continued to do the EOP wholeheartedly. I was also off and on with down-low relationship experiences. It became harder and harder to resist as the desires grew in my heart. I would say that in between those relationships I tried to stay away from the lifestyle. This cat and mouse game lasted until I was thirty-four years old. So anyway, in 2012, when I was thirty-two years of age. I was told that my brother, Lulu, had cancer as well as a few other health issues. The doctor told Mama G that they expected him to live for five to seven years. This made me really sad. A part of me felt okay. I thought maybe God had a different opinion. There were all these laws changing to help inmates who were minors at the time of their offense. I figured everything would be fine. I figured I'd get released soon enough to spend lots of quality time with him and make some great memories. I just knew God was gonna give us that after everything our family went through. I pretty much bet my heart and soul on it. That was in the bank, and it was nothing different anybody could tell me. I believed it with every fiber of my being.

Wow, it is hard to say this. In 2013, less than twelve whole months later, Mama G; Auntie Marie; my stepsister, Terri; and my stepdad, Speedy, all came to visit me on a Saturday morning. It was May 25. When I walked into the visiting room, everyone was looking up at me from the table they were assigned. No one would say anything at first. Mama G's eyes were watery, but she didn't speak. It seemed as though she couldn't. Finally, Auntie Marie looked me in my eyes while Mom held my hands, and she said to me, "Lulu is gone." I was in shock and disbelief. I just sat there, staring in a daze. I couldn't believe it. I was frozen. Time stopped. The tears wouldn't even fall from my eyes. I couldn't talk. I couldn't breathe. I couldn't swallow. I was told he died on May 22 at five forty-five in the morning. Apparently, his heart failed. The doctors spent all of Tuesday (May 21) night trying to get his blood pressure back up. Finally at 5:45 a.m. Wednesday morning, he was pronounced dead.

Once Mom finally was able to say something, she informed me Lulu's funeral would be the following week. She asked me to hurry up and write a poem so it could be read at his funeral by my cousin Larry (Marie's son). Anything else about the visit, I don't remember. It was a blur. Once visiting was over and I was sent back to my housing unit, that was when I had a bit of time alone and I cried the hardest tears I have ever cried in my life. I was tempted to scream, kick, punch something, just go as crazy as crazy could go. Instead I cried my eyes out. I wrote the poem that was going to be read at his funeral. I had to look upon the paper between teary, burning eyes. I'd never forget that day. That was seven years ago, and the pain had never left me. Before that, I only thought I knew pain, felt pain, was traumatized, felt alone and lost. What made things worse was the fact that I had to go it alone. My family all had one another to hold and console one another. I was in prison, where not a soul gave a damn about me. I had not a soul to wipe my tears or hold me upright when my legs were too weak to stand. It also appeared that at my darkest hour, God was nowhere to be found.

At that moment, I knew what true loneliness was. It appeared that my prayers fell upon deaf ears. As the days and weeks passed by, I lost my ability to function. I stopped doing my normal routine. I just wanted to stay in bed as much as possible. My ability to function and cope became so low that my psychologist referred me to a department state hospital. I stayed there for eleven months. In being honest, those eleven months saved my life. A therapeutic environment makes a huge difference. It's 90 percent not anything like prison. Maybe if you were a danger to people or yourself, you'd be sent to a lock-and-key environment. Where I was sent was peaceful. There was only one guard on the entire unit. The rest of the staff were all mental health staff and nurses and medical staff. There were forty of us patients, split up into eight small dorms. The therapy was very concentrated. There were lots of activities as well. The softness of that environment helped me get to a place where I could at least function again. It's safe to say I excelled there because the staff voted for me to be the unit's mentor. That gave me some responsibilities. Basically, when new patients came in, I had to show them the ropes. The staff would also tell patients they could confide in me, as there were times when mental health staff's shifts were over and the only ones there were medical staff. That did a lot for my self-esteem. At that hospital, I learned I was worth believing in. I was handpicked out of forty people, so there must be something good about me, right?

Some of the things I picked up in group sessions and one-on-one sessions were things like mindfulness, being assertive, ways to manage and minimize depression. I learned about boundaries. I learned what healthy relationships were. I was even able to spend some time addressing my sexuality. I opened up to the unit's psychologist about my confusion as well as the experiences I'd had. She said to me, "If that's who you are, then there's nothing wrong with that." She told me to stop making myself suffer and that I was torturing myself. She assured me there was nothing wrong with me just because I could possibly be that way. So I pondered the idea over time, and then something happened that gave me what I guess you could call a nudge. A young, very visible, and openly gay guy came to our unit. Me being the mentor, I had to tell him all the rules, show him what was behind every door, etc., etc. Oh my goodness, his youthful energy made me forget all about my problems when we were around each other. Nothing sexual, just two people laughing and giggling. We played Ping-Pong, talked, listened to music, horseplayed. It was totally chill. When the staff and patients saw us hanging out all the time, we brought a lot of attention to ourselves, especially me, because now people were wondering about me. Well, in the past, worried about what everyone thought, I would never have been that friendly with someone gay, but frankly I didn't give a damn anymore. When people stopped and looked, I noticed and looked back and just kept on doing what I was doing. Finally, one night in my dorm, I grew tired of everyone looking at me with those wandering eyes. I announced, "Look, guys, I've got something to tell y'all. I'm bisexual." To my surprise everyone was cool. Not one person switched up on me. I told them all I was gonna find out who my real friends were once I got back to the prison. I was anxious to come out to everyone I knew. I didn't exactly have any close friends or anything. There were just a bunch of guys I worked with in the print shop and the guys I played basketball with, but I was excited and looking forward to telling everyone who had ears. So my pleasant trip at the hospital was over after eleven months. I believe I was able to find a tremendous amount of guidance there, something I'd always be grateful for.

There is something I forgot to mention. Sixty-six days after Lulu passed away, my family informed me of my grandfather passing away. They told me during a visit, just as they had done with the news of Lulu's passing. At that point, I became nervous every time they came to see me, thinking they were going to give me the news of someone else's death. It took me a while to get past those fears.

Back to the time when I left the hospital. When I went back to the prison, I was so happy to come out and to openly associate myself with the LGBTQ community. With them was the first time I've ever felt like I fit in. I felt and still feel like this was who I was, and it was not a job. I didn't have to try. I simply just had to be. Don't get me wrong, this life was not without problems and headaches. Truth be told, I'd endured more hate and judgment than I'd ever imagined.

I'd never been laughed at the way I was laughed at. I'd never been discriminated against as much as I was now. Thing was, this was who I was 100 percent wholeheartedly, so come what may, I welcomed and embraced the good and bad. I gathered that when you're serious about something and you're passionate about it, with everything in your being, you'd die for it. You wouldn't shy away from challenges. You knew it wouldn't be easy, and you knew you'd be putting yourself in the spotlight, and you knew you'd have to grow thick skin. You'd also have to develop the ability to ignore the sideline. You would probably be like, "Now, hold on a minute. Someone who's just a bisexual guy doesn't go through all that." People figured that being bisexual wasn't that big of a deal. No one discriminated against someone who liked both sexes, not to some harsh degree. People felt like there was a class of people who had it the worst. Perhaps I'd agree. Just bear with me. My experiences when I returned to prison from the hospital started out as something like a fun ride for the first time in my life. I went up to all the gays and transgenders and told them I was finally able to admit that I was one of them. They embraced me, and I began to spend most of my free time with those who were now my people. Actually, they always were. I just fought against it for years.

I'd admit, some of the straight guys stopped socializing with me. The only people who would agree to be my cellmates at that point was someone gay. I didn't really let it get to me—well, not really. My excitement got a little out of hand in the beginning. I was probably too much of a social butterfly. That caused me to end up being involved in some messiness and drama. I was unaware of this side of the gay crowd. Me being a very sensitive person, I started isolating myself from people. Unfortunately, when I withdraw and isolate, I become my own worst enemy. I became depressed, and daily my depression got worse. This state of mind also left me vulnerable to people who liked to pounce on others when they were isolated and wounded. This guy by the name of Ray must've had noticed something about me, because he started being really nice to me, showing a lot of concern, and giving me little gifts. He said I looked sad, and he didn't like to see me like that. As the days passed by, he spoiled me, and I grew very familiar with him. We became an item despite that weird feeling in my gut and despite other people telling me he was no good. Back then I guess my self-esteem wasn't where it was supposed to be. I didn't think or believe I was worthy of an awesome person. I basically accepted the first person that gave me their attention and time. He started out really sweet, and he did a really good job of catering to me. After a few months passed by, he became extremely possessive. He controlled my every move. He didn't want me to have friends as he kept trying to poison me against people. He didn't allow me to walk anywhere alone. Once I got a job, he'd be waiting for me right outside my job. I was in a prison inside of a prison. Finally, I worked up enough nerve to start to try to pull away from him. I started spending time with a few of the gays. He did not like that whatsoever. On December 18, 2015, Ray and I had been together for about one year. It was on a Friday afternoon. A group of correctional officers came looking for me. Once they found me, I was handcuffed and taken to the program office. There, I was locked inside this small cage. I was told that I was going to ad seg / the hole. An officer came and read to me what was called a lockup order. The order said back in October of 2015, an anonymous inmate witnessed me groping another inmate outside in the yard area. First of all, let me tell you, administration took that sort of thing very seriously. I tried to tell the officer that was impossible because the job where I work had me there all day. I hardly ever had a chance to come to the yard. I explained to him that at work we clocked in and out. He could check with my boss, and my boss would verify me being at work on the day in question.

Well, the officer didn't seem to care. He just said to be patient and let it come out in the investigation. He said they had no choice but to take me to the hole. Let me tell you, I went absolutely crazy. I had worked so hard over the years, did so much maturing, learning, growing, everything I could to turn my reputation around. I felt in that moment as if all my hard work went down the drain. No one was ever gonna believe a word I say now about how much I've changed. I panicked. In those few seconds, I came to the conclusion even if I was ever fortunate enough to get a parole hearing, for the possibility of being paroled, it was all over for me now. This was definitely the angriest I'd ever been in my whole life. I must've blacked out. I started banging my head against the metal cage, fast and nonstop. Blood ran down my face and all over my shirt. The captain, the LT, sergeants, and a bunch of officers were all around the cage begging me to calm down. I was cursing at them, saying "Fuck you!" I didn't care. I wanted to die, and I didn't care what anybody said.

At least that's what I said at that moment, but really I was just scared. I didn't want to kill myself. I was worried this would ruin my chances even more. What sucks was that I had no idea whom I supposedly harmed. So once I calmed down, I received medical attention. Then I was put on suicide watch for two weeks. My head was busted open pretty badly. They just put some butterfly stitches on my forehead and sent me on my way. If they had given me regular stiches, my scar probably would look better than it looked right now. After two weeks, I was sent to the hole for three weeks. For the entire five weeks total, I was considered ad seg status, even while in suicide watch. After the five weeks were up, I was told the investigation revealed the accusations were unwarranted. There was no victim, and they didn't know who wrote the note. I had no idea either, at first. Ray was sending me all these messages in the hole saying a group of gay guys whom I was friends with all turned on me. He said they were behind the mysterious note that was put inside the staff's box. He asked people to check on me a lot. I started believing he was the only one who really cared for me. Even though he treated me bad often, he really had my back. When I was released from the hole, I told all the gays to stay the fuck away from me. He was the only person I wanted to be around. When he told me he was constantly talking to staff, trying to help me and vouch for me, I believed him.

I continued being with him. It lasted for maybe two months, and his treatment of me turned even uglier than before. I begged him to please leave me alone. I told him I didn't want to be with him anymore. This time I actually had the courage to tell mental health staff and officers that he wouldn't stop harassing me. No one did anything about it, though. I started aggressively pulling away from him this time. I started getting in his face, telling him to leave me alone. He said "Okay, fine," and switched to a different cell on a different floor. However, he still kept creeping up on me, saying weird things to me (basically calling me messed-up names). The next thing I knew, here came the officers again looking for me. What did you know, it was another note. This time, instead of putting me in a cage, they took me into the LT's office, and we talked. He showed me the note and asked me if I had any idea what this was all about.

I replied, "I believe I know who is behind all this." An officer jumped into the conversation, and once I said I believed it was Ray, this particular officer asked the LT to hold on (as far as sending me to the hole again) while he searched the other inmate's cell (Ray) for a handwriting sample. The officer took the note with him. A little while later, he returned saying the handwriting on the note and the handwriting found on things in Ray's cell were a match.

This time, they listened to me. They took Ray to the hole and let me go. Days later, I was called to the program office to speak with the LT. He had me read the report saying Ray harassed me and falsified charges against me. He told me to sign on the bottom of the paper if I was satisfied with the findings or if there was anything else I wanted to add concerning my relationship with him. Thank goodness at least one officer gave me the benefit of the doubt and the truth came out. I felt so stupid and naive not realizing at first that the person I was with meant me so much harm, all because I no longer wanted to be in an abusive relationship. It appeared his mindset was if he couldn't have me, no one could. I mean, if he would've treated me right, I wouldn't have been trying to get away from him.

To pour salt in the wound, after Ray was gone to the hole for a few days already, an officer pulled me to the side and said it wasn't right what he did to me. He said Ray had been at that prison for many years already. He said he'd done these crazy things to young gays time and time again. He called him a predator. He said that when Ray got out of the hole, he was gonna be right back at it, wherever he ended up. If so many people knew this, why didn't anyone ever tell me these things before in the beginning? People only said they didn't like him and he was no good. When I asked them how and why he was no good, they never gave me straight answers.

The officer that pulled me over to talk said that I overreacted when I busted my head open after having a note dropped on me the first time. He said I should've stayed calm and just let the process play out. My response to that was it should have never happened in the first place. Perhaps I overreacted. I'm not gonna lie, I did lose control. I was more scared and angry than I would've ever imagined (under any circumstances).

It was the worst feeling in the world. When it came to doing something wrong, if I'd done something wrong, then okay, I couldn't cry about being held accountable or responsible, but to suffer at the hands of a false accusation was an unbearable thing for me. This wasn't like a situation where you'd get arrested for a crime you didn't commit, and you'd get the best lawyer possible and put your trust in the justice system and where you get your day in court. No, me, you see, when I was seventeen years old, I did some horrible things to two innocent people who didn't deserve it. I'd been busting my ass to rehabilitate in a system that wasn't always conducive for someone in pursuit of change and growth or maturity. This environment was negative where for each good accomplishment, you get two or three encounters that plant ugly seeds, such as, "You're nothing but scum" and "Here's my foot on your neck."

Regardless, I'd done my damnedest to overcome all things. It had not been easy. Some really stupid choices brought upon me. No possible hope for a future. Don't get me wrong. I'd witnessed quite a few people be granted a second chance. It just hadn't happened for me yet. It looked as if I'd possibly had a chance when new laws were passed concerning juvenile offenders. This had happened once every blue moon. And once every blue moon, doors were slammed in my face.

I freaked out on December 18, 2015, because even if I was fortunate enough to ever go before a parole board anytime soon, it would be extremely difficult to obtain parole being granted. However, if I did anything wrong or got in any trouble, it would pretty much become impossible. Then either I'd die in prison or get released at such an old age that I'd have no meaningful life left.

At this time it was 2020. I was now forty years old. Since the last incident I spoke of, I'd transferred to a few different prisons due to my security level dropping, which was based on good programming.

I'd gotten a lot smarter about not getting involved with the wrong people and staying away from negative people. For some reason, I kept holding on. I hadn't had any more episodes of self-harm or suicide attempts. I believed in my heart I owed it to myself to keep going just in case there was a slim possibility of me seeing a second chance, a chance of living at least a taste of a good-quality life. I don't believe many people believed I'd be the person I am today—soft-spoken, compassionate, honest, trustworthy, thoughtful, considerate, responsible, and more than anything, remorseful. I lived every day righting my wrongs and making amends for my past. As for my mental health status, I definitely knew for a fact that if it weren't for the mental health program, I wouldn't have healed, and I wouldn't be who I am today. However, I must say, I defied the odds. I was told by a few psychiatrists that my chemical imbalance would make it impossible for me to function without medication. Well, I began to question that because the medication helped me for a little while, then I'd go back to being really depressed. They'd have to keep upping my dosage. It worked for a while, then it wore off, and so on and so forth. At some point, it began feeling like I was just messing my body and my mind up because my depression kept coming back. Every time I felt good, it was temporary. The things that really helped me were the groups, therapy, getting older, opening up my eyes, gaining some understanding. I began to come to terms with how life was, figuring out how to find meaning. I was figuring out who I was, why I was the way I was, and what I could do about it. I had to ask others and myself tough questions. I still hadn't completely figured out what was going on with my identity, even though I had come out, because in time I was still having issues. When I was thirty-seven years old, I finally understood, and I finally was able to admit to myself I'd never felt comfortable in this body. I was born in the wrong body. I remember saying to a transgender friend named Mia one day that I believed I might be transgender. She was pretty surprised because she never saw it coming. I hadn't talked about it. I just spent time with several transgender friends for months every single day. I felt 100 percent at home, and I thought about all the things I'd been through trying to figure me out. No one influenced me. They didn't even try. It's just that with time, I was so comfortable, I was so at one with them, and it was so natural. I thought like them, I felt like them. Their spirit and my spirit fit the same shoes. I felt as though it was us and then everyone else.

For one whole year, I had to fight tooth and nail to be approved for hormone replacement therapy. It was hard for me to get it because of my mental health history, but I stayed with it. Now, I'd been receiving hormone replacement therapy for two years. I guess you could say I'd fought two battles and won. I'd helped the woman in me fight her way into existence.

But first, I had to tend to the traumatized child inside me, who himself became the monster. Truth be told, I had to nurture them both every single day, perhaps for the rest of my life. This would keep me on the right track. I was grateful to the universe. I'd learned how to live. I'd learned how to love. I'd learned how to be loved. I'd learned how to treat myself. I'd learned what was decent and what was not. I'd learned how to have integrity. I'd learned the importance and significance of making a positive difference in people's lives.

I believe I'd gained the respect of the people who were in my life today. They probably felt they had no choice. After all, I'd accomplished things no one thought I could. I survived things I probably should not have survived. One day at a time, I was thriving. I had been off psychiatric medication for four and a half years now. I was completely out of the mental health program. After seven years and a lot of work, my doctors agreed that I was ready. They believed I could function, even in the outside world, if given the chance.

As far as the outside world was concerned, after all this time, after almost giving up, after so many doors being slammed shut, I'd finally have a chance to be paroled in the near future. For those who support me, please keep your fingers crossed. There would be no guarantees. In life, there hardly ever would be. Lots of people would never see better days after a life of suffering. Millions of these people never did anything to deserve their suffering. Think about the people who endured slavery, the people who'd been kidnapped and kept against their will for many years. Many of them were born into it and died in it. They didn't do anything wrong. What about the family who had to do only God knows what to have food on their table? What about the child walking down the street to or from school who was victimized by some sick person or a stray bullet? What about the person who had worked hard their entire life, never done anything to hurt or harm anyone, and then lost everything? So many people suffer. Who was I to cry about my suffering? What gave me the right to inflict pain on someone else who might be hurting just as much as me? I wished this was a question I never had to be in a position to ask myself. Unfortunately, I put myself in that kind of a position. It took me years to finally be able to ask myself these questions. I felt foolish about thinking the world was picking on me. I felt that way because I wasn't paying attention to what other people were going through. I was selfish, and I was a coward. I didn't think about anyone else, just me. To be honest, I didn't even do that part right, because when someone was really thinking about themself in the right kind of way, as in they loved themselves, they wouldn't stoop down to or give in to animal behavior. They would know that hurting someone was not human behavior. It was animal behavior, and it was savage behavior. When I was twenty-nine, I made up my mind that I didn't want to be that person anymore. I knew it wouldn't be an easy thing, because once someone crossed that line of what was morally decent and what wasn't, it was pretty hard to make it back. Me, on the other hand, I vowed to make it back or die trying.

When I was twenty-two, I didn't think I could make it back. That was why I attempted suicide. I was hopeless, and I saw no light at the end of the tunnel. I thought there was no way I could recover. I thought I was a lost cause. But I began to see things, feel things, and learn about things that made me believe. It was funny how life was. I did all kinds of things trying to get my family to be more supportive and involved in my life. I spent a lot of time feeling sorry for myself in the process. Once I worked on myself, matured, and grew into the person I was supposed to be, the love and the respect I had from the people in my life today blew my mind. All I had to do was get myself together. I just had to work hard, really hard, and I saw the world couldn't help but to respect and acknowledge it.

When you're doing the right thing in life, being productive, making a difference, building positive and healthy relationships, life is beautiful. Even here where I was, I got to experience a bit of peace now because of where I've been, because of what I know, and because of my level of acceptance, and I'd lived to tell about it. I was humbled. I was loved and supported by some beautiful human beings. If I would never isolate myself or stray way, I could and I would stay on the path to goodness. I was not sure about other people, but I couldn't afford to isolate myself, because that was a negative trigger for me. A certain level of pains, hurts, scars, and depressions still remained with me to a degree. It was just that I'd picked up tools that helped me to manage things better. There was also probably always gonna be a level of regrets and feeling bad about the people I'd harmed. There was no way I could ever possibly forget about those incidents.

In life there were constant reminders, and each time I felt bad all over again. In those moments, I always had to have self-talks with myself, reminding me of what I've been doing with the rest of my life. I was making it right, and I was giving back. Every day I was living a life of making amends.

In My Big Brother's Arms (5/25/13)

I remember when we were little
And the times were cold,
We were so, so far away
From Mama's loving home.
I had a face full of tears
And a runny nose
In the midst of nights
That were dark and long,
But I had you.

You'd put your arms around me
And wouldn't let me go
Until I fell asleep,
Telling me, "Little brother,
It's gonna be all right,"
Though you cried the same tears
And shared my fears.
I got through hell
Because you were near.
In my heart you will
Always be dear.
And even though I know
I'll see you when I get there,
Where angels reside,
I wish you would've had the chance
To see me living an ideal life,
As in a far cry
From these chains and strife,
But I assure you with my right
Hand to God,
I'm different now, truly a man of God.

Sorry, big brother,
That in your last days,
I was unable to hold
You in my arms
As you did for me,
But I'm sure God has you
Somewhere safe and warm.

I will always love you,
And I promise to always be the best I can be.
You watch, I'll make you proud.

Sincerely,
Your little brother

Memories and Moments (2013)

You left, how I wish you could've stayed.
Oh, how I miss the way we played.
When we were young,
We encountered some hard times,
But at times some fun,
Like playing ball in the sun,
Or running around on the beach.
Oh, yeah, remember when
We raced each other
Down the street,
Laughing like birds and free,
Horseplaying in the living room.
Big bro, I miss you.

I had no idea you'd be leaving soon. I feel as though
When I return home, it's to a lifeless
And empty room.
But I'll hold onto these memories and moments
Like precious jewels.
I'll never forget your face, your voice, or your smile.
I hope to see your appearance in at least one of my future children,
Anything to keep a part of you living.

God knows there will forever be
A part of me missing.

Yeah, maybe in spirit,
But physically I no longer have a brother,
And it hurts like nobody knows.

Perhaps like a sword through my soul,
Oh, where will I go
When I wanna know
Of a big brother's advice
About things in my life
In the midst of trying to live right?
I guess I'll just turn out the lights
And silently listen for whispers
In the quiet of the night.

Hey, God (Dedicated to My Creator)

In a world surrounded by danger,
Millions of men full of rage and anger.
At times to keep my peace and piece of mind,
I often find myself in solitude,
Not to be rude,
But sometimes it's for the better,
Because people change
More often than the weather.
Even when in darkness I smile,
Because I know
You won't let me see
More than I can bear.
It's more than comforting
To know that you'll always be here,
Regardless of the fact
That it seems as though
At times I don't care
If I do right or wrong.
But I've finally realized
That without you,
I can't carry on.

Untitled

Sometimes I'm scared of love,
But I just can't resist.
It appears that to jump in blindfolded,
My heart persists.

This place in which they call love,
For me, it is so intense.

Time after time,
Rain, tears, and scars
In the midst of my fears,
That I'll fall.
God's kid, he calls.
Late at night,
When the world's on pause,
On his knees and paws. He's weak, he crawls.

Part spirit, part flesh.
A percentage is good,
Also I'm partly a mess.
But I do my best,
To love you at all.
But for some reason
Still, one day you're gone,
Like my favorite song.
It only lasted for a few moments,
Though I begged it
To last all night long.

It faded away and left me all alone.

Peace (12/15/2015)

The more we chase material possessions,
Does peace escape us?
Does peace escape us?

When we meddle in others' affairs,
Is it still possible to maintain peace?

When we worry about our past or
A day yet to come, is peace possible?

When we stress until our hair abandons us,
Are we living in peace?

When we don't see each other as one race,
Is peace possible?
Is peace possible?

If we allow our differences to separate us, are we living in peace?

I wonder if peace is even possible.

Untitled (1/26/2016)

Here's something that's so funny,
I've had the most fun with no money.

Like having a water fight
During July's hottest nights (and days).

But for money, I must warn
Men from all over start wars.

For me, more suitable is something simple,
Like fighting off a puppy that likes to kiss you.
I'm taking it all in while I still can, before I'm somewhere beneath
the ocean and
The sand.
Just where, no one really knows,
Where what remains of us all goes.
(Not for a fact.)

Feel My Pain (2006)

Trapped inside these walls
With nothin' but my fears.
At night in my solitude,
I wrestle with my tears.
No way in hell could I
Ever imagine this slavery
For this many years.

They say the Lord is always near,
Especially when you fall.
Well, I've fallen, and fallen hard.
Where are you, God?
I need you here.

I'm a twenty-six-year-old man with many different minds.
One day I have the patience
To move forward enduring what I must,
Having faith in your promises,
Which requires my total trust.
But at times, I'm mentally weak
And wanna resort to suicide,
But I worry for my mama,
And there's also my pride.
Maybe I'd care less
If a tragedy came too soon
And she was to die.

One of my legs and one of my arms
Are already broken
Because my pops isn't around.
When witnessing father-and-son relationships,
I bow my head and focus all my attention to the ground.

God knows
I'm trying my best to stay strong,
But onto hardly anything
Do I have to hang on.

A Life-Threatening Pain (2012)

So many lives shattered
Because of so much blood splattered,
But I've always assumed
That life does matter.

More pain than a little bit.
Today a stray bullet
Blew out the brains of a little kid.
When I heard the news,
I felt like drinking a little bit
To get rid of it.
I'm talking about
The heartache that hit my soul.
Man, I'm sick of this.

Jail cells and war stories.
As soon as I'm free,
You'll know about me,
And you'll see me giving God glory.
How I was sentenced to life,
But the Lord had something better in mind for me.

A world filled with so much hate
Doesn't decide my fate.
My life is in the hands
Of the one whose son died for me.

For thirteen years you've chipped in
With your side,
Now hear my story.

Once upon a time
My skinny wrists
Were chained,

And that night it rained.
Or perhaps that was just my pain
In the form of tears.

Since then I've been locked in a spot
That's not much bigger than a mailbox.
I've been kicked while down
And shell-shocked.
When given this time
Doing it, I said,
"No, the hell I'm not.
I wouldn't dare."
Do sixty-six years
Not because I'm tough as nails
But because I couldn't bear
Being buried alive in concrete
Layer upon layer.

In the midst of my struggles
I've attempted suicide,
But God wouldn't let me go.
He's healed my wounds
And touched my soul.

For many, many years,
I've wanted to give up.
It appeared as though I had no chance of recovery
But thank God for loving me
Because now it looks
Like I have a real chance at going home.

The same guy who once was neglected,
Beaten, afraid, and alone.

(In 2012, that was one of the many times I thought I had a chance,
only to have a door slammed in my face. I wrote this poem thinking
I finally had a shot.)

Untitled (8/18/2015)

For me,
Life is bad dreams
And butterflies.

Bittersweet,
Quite worth the fight.
Wanna try?

Forever young
Is the tune
Of my spirit.

Mature and dumb,
My mind's room.
The pictures, vivid.

Infinity (8/25/2015)

Infinity is my love for family
Also those only friends to me.

Infinity seems the ocean's distance,
Its force knows no resistance.

For infinity we walk the earth.
Once done, we return to dirt

Infinity describes the sky.
Infinity equals my cries.

Infinity describes a bird's wings.
Infinity describes songs we sing.

Infinity equates deepness of souls.
Infinity relates belief to goals.

To infinity we travel
While our dreams are unraveled.
Infinity has no end.
Mother Nature, my friend.

Earthquake (2015)

Water drowns my soul,
Travels up my nose.
Falling debris
Scars my flesh
And bloodies my clothes.
If and when it gets better,
Only my creator knows.

Buildings shake
And grounds rattle,
My thirty-five years of existence
Have been an earthquake
That has me rattled.
But still I stand.
I continue to learn,
Grow, and give back
In my estimation.
This simply makes me human,
No greater or lesser
Than any other.

Untitled (2015)

Her eyes were like an evil spirit
Deceptively snatching my soul,
Only to crush me.

My heart is like fragile glass,
Easily shattered
And should be handled with care.

Fall is like a holiday.
Time to snuggle closely
With loved ones.

My feet are like bricks,
Making it difficult for me
To put one in front of the other.

My heart is like a small child,
Naive and too trusting
In such a cold world.

Breathe (10/13/2015)

As though it's over, sometimes it seems.
However, I'll continue to breathe.

There are occasions where I want to bow out
And throw in the towel,
But the warrior inside lets out a howl
And tells me to stop and think,
To simply close my eyes and deeply breathe.

So though my chest is scarred,
I'm not completely marred.
And though shit gets hard,
It seems I'll choose to breathe.

To Me and You (2/22/2016)

May you always have purpose,
A reason to move forward,
And someone to show compassion toward.
May you effortless find reasons to smile
And laughter easily find you, like it does a small child.
In old age, may your bones not ache
Beyond what you can bear.
May you never experience loneliness
Or the lack of at least one friend who cares.

May I Find and Keep Peace (2016)

May I find and keep peace
And leave alone the many ups and downs.
One moment happy-go-lucky,
The next, tears and frowns.

Instead of a second opinion and medication,
May I be able to depend on God and meditation.

May I learn to mentally find myself alone
Next to the ocean,
Becoming one with nature
Forming a beautiful closeness.

May I always have the energy to keep going,
And may I continue reading so that I can keep knowing.

For Hilary Swank (3/15/2016)

From a trailer park to Hollywood,
Where I come from,
We call that so hood.

She reminds me of Tupac's poetry,
A rose that grew from concrete.
Stemming from sleeping in a car,
Parked on a dark street.

So much like me, an oddball.
Having ADHD and fitting in with no crowds,
As many labeled you crazy,
But you still became a million-dollar baby.

So much more relatable when a star
Comes from humble beginnings.
It touches me deeply
When I know we've both lived it.

My Spirit Cries (2016)

Trying to find God in a foggy maze.
In need of a cleansing, a soul that's rotten.
Sort of young, but feeling old and forgotten.
Kiss my wounds and touch my inner scars.

My spirit cries
Seeking guidance.
My spirit cries
Seeking comfort.
My spirit cries
Because I've forgotten what love is.
My spirit cries
Because my life's a mess.
Some will preach that in a way,
I'm blessed.
I'm sure even the dead can attest
As I beg to differ.
Arguing and envying them
That they now can rest.
No longer having to wade in the water.

Pain (2/14/2018)

When I call to mind my closest friend,
I think of pain.
Like long, dark nights filled with nothingness
And rain.

When times turn tragic,
Pain is my next of kin.

When my spirits are high,
Pain has a way of knocking me
Out of the sky,
And pain could care less
How hard I cry.
No, pain cares less about my bloodshot eyes.
Pain takes pleasure in the times,
A relative, a friend, even a lover
Has told me lies.

Pain overtakes us all,
When someone dear suddenly dies.
And when it's my time,
I have a funny feeling that pain will be there
Just in the nick of time.

Addiction and Freedom (2/28/2018)

Having a choice is a form of freedom.
If I choose to be addicted,
Am I as free as I believe
Because I'm relieved
From all my stress?
While the fog blinds my eyes
To my life being a mess.
Who cares?
Because all the smoke in my chest
Is the best
My world has ever had to offer.

I once knew another way,
But I lost it.
My hand held a precious jewel,
But somewhere along the way,
I dropped it.
That is, hypothetically speaking.
Truthfully speaking, I'm free.
Because finally, I'm simply me.

Pain and Beauty (3/7/2018)

I've longed for something
That was not there.
So when I witness a lonely soul,
I care.

The bruises and lashes
Isn't quite what an innocent child is asking
Concerning his or her dreams
I've been there too,
And I've survived
Which I believe proves I'm strong.
I'm sure a naysayer couldn't prove me wrong,
But woe is man,
Despite his plans.

Fortunately for us all,
Life's not
Completely bad.
There's things that make us laugh
And things that make our hearts glad.

Home (3/14/2018)

Home sweet home.
I'm not sure I've ever had one.
It's safe to say
I've never been my dad's son.

While I can think of a thousand places
I've laid my head,
Had a hot meal,
And made my bed,
Was it home?
Where with a dozen voices,
I felt alone.
Trails of tears on each side of my nose,
Blood in my shoes,
And rips in my clothes.
When I can count
Each hug on five fingers,
When I find my companionship
In the words
And the voice of a singer.
Perhaps the only home I have
Is in my dreams.
And as crazy as this sounds,
I still believe.

Death (3/28/2018)

Death to you,
That old part of me
I never agreed with,
That lie I never believed in.

Death to the previous
Images in the mirror.
As time passes,
Gladly,
The truth will become clearer.

Death to the unspoken sin
Of living in someone else's skin.
Besides my own.

I'm not speaking of death
That buries us in the ground.
I'm speaking of forsaking being tossed to and fro
On life's merry-go-round.

Putting your foot down,
Letting your fist pound
In protest,
Demanding yourselves best,
Lest you die
To be only your true self.

Slowly Fading (3/28/2018)

There are times I feel strong and amazing,
But deep down I also know
That I'm slowly fading.
You'd see a few grays
If I weren't always shaving.

I can jump, run,
And kinda dance.
I don't have many problems
Trying to find romance and dating,
But if I stop moving
Long enough to ponder,
I remember I'm slowly fading.

How about that
For a piece of humble pie?
No, I won't run and cry,
I'll just be mindful and enjoy the sky
And get high
On my little bit of life,
And love love,
Whether husband or wife.

My Mama

I could care less about fame and fortune.
I care more about the stars and the sunrise
Or the look in a proud mother's eyes.

In accordance with the Bible's description,
I'm convinced she's an angel in disguise,
Loving me despite my faults
Regardless of the pain I caused
Putting her life on pause
To check on the welfare of her baby.
Seeing something special in me
When the rest of the world labeled me crazy,
And though I'm now grown
And my days of youth are gone,
I feel safe when you hug me and
Kiss me on the cheek.
Your soft words of wisdom and concern
Are comforting like a quilt,
Soothing like a hummingbird's song
And cool like a summer breeze
That rocks me to sleep.

A Poem for Mama G

Words almost always fail to describe
How much you touch my soul.
I've always regretted my past mistakes,
The things I did long ago.
But truth be told,
Feeling bad, alone, didn't change me.
The relationship and love we've developed
Helped me most to grow,
In regard to how every female
Should be treated and viewed.
It's crazy how
All you have ever wanted
Was the best of me
When the world was cold
And had the rest for me.
But it was just too hard for a while
For me to see it through my pain and trauma.

Now I can honestly say that despite some of our
Past history, you're one hell of a mama.
Lovely, wonderful, beautiful, human, and entitled to mistakes.
There's just so much to love about you.
I will forever see a woman differently because of the way I see you.
It took me a while to get it, but you remained patient.
Mama, thank you for waiting. I'll take this lesson with me every-
where I go
For the rest of my life.

Happy Mother's Day.

About the Author

I WAS ONCE TOLD BY AN EX TO TURN TRAGEDY INTO TRIUMPH. THIS ADVICE HAS BEEN AN ADDED SEED AMONGST THE MANY SEEDS THAT WERE PLANTED OVER THE YEARS. AS I WAS HEALING FROM THE SCARS AND THE UGLINESS OF THE PAST, THESES SEEDS HAD THE NECESSARY ROOM TO GROW. WHAT I'VE LEARNED ALONG THE WAY IS THAT SOMETHING BEAUTIFUL AND SPLENDID CAN COME OF UGLINESS,IN SPITE OF ONES BLEMISHES. WITHIN REASON,ALL THINGS ARE POSSIBLE.

I'd like to thank all the wonderful people in my life today. You all show me every day that beauty is possible. If anyone wishes to contact me, here's my information.

ericamoseley21@gmail.com